CAS

HEROES AT HEART

MARYANN JORDAN

ISBN ebook: 978-1-947214-52-1

ISBN print: 978-1-947214-53-8

Created with Vellum

Author's Note

Please remember that this is a work of fiction. I have lived in numerous states as well as overseas, but for the last twenty years have called Virginia my home. I often choose to use fictional city names with some geographical accuracies.

These fictionally named cities allow me to use my creativity and not feel constricted by attempting to accurately portray the areas.

It is my hope that my readers will allow me this creative license and understand my fictional world.

I also do quite a bit of research on my books and try to write on subjects with accuracy. There will always be points where creative license will be used in order to create scenes or plots.

DEDICATION

As an adolescent counselor for over twenty-five years, I had the opportunity to work with many young people. One young man, upset over a poor choice he had made, came to me. As I listened to his story and his confession, I told him that the true measure of a man was not in the mistakes he made, but in how he handled those mistakes. I remember the look on his face when I told him I was sure he was going to be a good man.

So this series is dedicated to all the students over the years who allowed me to be a part of their lives.

1

I wonder who is moving in across the street...

The autumn day was hot and sunny, and Miss Ethel stood at her front door, knowing that her boys would soon be getting off the school bus. Activity across the street had captured her interest for most of the day, and she watched as movers made continuous trips back and forth from a small moving van to the inside of the house.

There was only one other car in the driveway, and a man and a young girl alighted from the vehicle. The man walked directly into the house, stopping only to talk to one of the moving men, but the girl had skipped around the front yard, hopping with excitement and dancing with what appeared to be absolute delight.

Miss Ethel chuckled aloud at the girl's antics. It had not escaped her notice over the years that young girls often exhibited an uninhibited sense of self... until they became older. They laughed when they wanted to laugh. Danced when they wanted to dance. Sang when they wanted to sing.

She had been blessed with all boys but knew that if God had gifted her with a girl first, that was what she would have taken in. She waited for a few seconds to see if regret would slide through her, but it did not.

"Oh, George, I still sometimes wonder what our lives would have been like if we had had children." Her husband had died many years ago, but she still talked to him, taking comfort in his Heavenly presence. At the time he passed, she had searched for a new purpose in life, and by chance overheard a conversation at her church about the need for foster families. That not only gave her a purpose but changed her irrevocably.

The little girl twirling in her front yard across the street recaptured Miss Ethel's attention, and her smile widened.

"Somewhere over the rainbow..."

The little girl was now singing at the top of her lungs. She was a tiny thing with sleek black hair, and Miss Ethel wondered her age. *It's so hard to tell nowadays... some of my boys already look like men.*

The years had passed quicker than she had wanted. Zander was now a junior in high school with the others in grades just below him, ending with Asher, Zeke, and Cas in eighth grade.

The little girl ran inside her house, and just as Miss Ethel was turning from the door, the school bus stopped at the corner, letting out the middle and high school students who lived in the neighborhood. She watched as all eight of her boys walked down the street together, coming up the driveway as they neared the house. "Oh, my, George. Look how handsome they all are."

As was her daily habit, she stepped out onto the porch to greet them at the end of the school day. A slight breeze ruffled her dress, and she was struck with the thought that the winds of time were passing quickly.

Change was not always easy, but it came whether we wanted it to or not. Miss Ethel had certainly lived long enough to know how true that was. She had lived for many years without the sounds of children in her home and knew that there would be many years of solitude after they left. She was smart enough to know what was inevitable and honest enough to know that it would be painful. *"To say goodbye is to die a little."* The quote from Raymond Chandler ran through her mind and she sighed. Pushing those thoughts to the side, she smiled as each of her boys greeted her warmly, almost in unison.

"Hello, boys," she called out, a hug offered to each of them. "Cookies are just out of the oven, so have a snack."

"Chocolate chip oatmeal?"

"Now, Cas. What do you think?"

Laughing, he said, "I know that's our favorite, so I'll bet that's what you made."

"Go on in and find out," she said, her eyes twinkling. All eight boys passed by her as they made their way down the hall and into the kitchen.

Their routine was well established. She would listen as they talked about their day, loving every moment of hearing what they had done, what they had learned, and, most importantly, what they thought. They were growing up, and, like any mother, she felt the pride and the pangs of that maturation.

Hearing the boys in the dining room with their snacks, she blinked, realizing she was still standing at the front door. With another glance across the street, she spied the little girl once more in the yard twirling.

Change was coming... she could feel it with the breeze. A slow smile curved her lips. *Sometimes, change is good.*

Castiel Holtz sat in the shade of one of the large trees in the front yard. At thirteen years old he would be considered by many to be too old to just sit under a tree, but his family never made him feel self-conscious about his habit. His brothers were practicing their pitches in the back yard where they had plenty of room, but he preferred the small copse of trees that were in the front corner of the yard. Sitting on the moss, the earthy scent rose up to meet him.

He used the time to whittle, picking up any stick that was available and watching the wood change as the knife blade scraped over its surface. The knife had belonged to his father, one of the few things that he had left.

Sitting under the trees was also where he remembered his family's house in the woods. He remembered his father's workshop, filled with various saws, planers, routers, sanders, and all the other items needed to turn pieces of wood into beautiful pieces of furniture. He remembered the burning smell as the electric saw sliced through the wood. He remembered the way the wood would curl in little bits as his father moved the planer over its surface.

Memories, a few pictures, and his father's pocketknife were all he had left of his parents. Senseless violence had ripped everything else away from him. As time went by, it was sometimes harder and harder to remember. Perhaps that was why he enjoyed the quiet time whittling in the corner of the yard.

The first time Miss Ethel found him whittling, his heart had pounded in fear that she would take his knife away.

She had smiled and said, "What a lovely knife. My father and my husband always carried a knife in their pocket. Back then, most men had one."

He was surprised she did not get upset, considering his earlier foster homes had forbidden him to have a knife. "My dad liked to whittle and carve."

Miss Ethel had clapped her hands in joy and said, "Oh, my father loved to whittle also! You will have to show me some of the work you do."

He had breathed a sigh of relief, remembering how his first foster mother had screamed at the sight of him holding the knife, sure that he was going to hurt someone. He had hidden the knife, lying when asked about it later, telling them he lost it. He was in two more foster homes after that and kept his father's pocketknife secret both times, not willing for someone to take it from him.

Miss Ethel was different. She allowed him to work

with the wood whenever he wanted to, always impressed with whatever he created.

Shouts were heard from the back yard, and he smiled. *Zander probably hit a home run... or at least hit it over the back fence.*

"Whatcha doing?"

Startled out of his private musings, his eyes jerked open wide as his head swung around toward the sidewalk at the sound of a high-pitched voice. Just on the other side of the fence stood a dark-haired little girl. With him sitting on the ground, her face was partially hidden by the slats in the picket fence. He did not recognize her, but, irritated that she had disturbed his quiet, he wanted her to leave him alone. Shrugging, he turned back to his whittling, dismissing her with a one-word answer. "Nothing."

She huffed loudly. "I can see you're not doing *nothing*. You've got a knife. What are you making?" Her face was pressed close to the fence slats so she could peek through.

"Why is it any of your business?" he fired back, jumping to his feet. Now that he was standing and could see over the fence, he had a better look at her. Her hair was black, trimmed to just above her shoulders, and held back from her face with a blue headband. He had no idea how old she was, but even though she was small, he now thought she was older than he had originally assumed.

Her face was pale as though she did not play out in the sun very often, but he had to admit it was pretty. Not pretty like the eighth-grade girls in his class who wore makeup and most of whom giggled too much but already had boobs and hips that made all the eighth-grade boys take notice. This girl was too young for him to have those thoughts, but she was pretty, nonetheless.

She continued to stare at him with large, blue eyes, tilting her head slightly as she smiled. "My name's Bianca," she said. She twisted her head and glanced to the house across the street and said, "We just moved there today. Me and my dad. We used to live on the other side of town in an apartment, but Dad wanted me to have a house and a neighborhood to play in."

It was on the tip of his tongue to say he did not care what her name was or where she lived, but when she did not mention a mom, he took notice. He deflated as the desire to be rude left him. "My name is Cas." He waited for the inevitable question about his name, but she simply smiled again.

"Cas. I like that. Is it short for something?"

Jaw tight, he admitted, "Castiel. It's short for Castiel."

Eyes wide, she smiled wider. "Oh, I really like your name." Her blue eyes twinkled, and she bounced on her toes. "How old are you?"

He opened his mouth then snapped it closed again. She kept staring, so he finally answered. "Thirteen."

"I'm eleven."

Her age surprised him because of her small stature.

She clapped her hands at his wide-eyed surprise. "I know. I'm little. Dad says my mom was little, too."

Once again, he noted that her mom was mentioned in past tense and wondered about Bianca's family.

More shouts could be heard from the back yard, and her brows lowered slightly as she asked, "Who's that?"

"You've got a lot of questions."

"Yes, but how can you find out anything unless you ask questions?"

It did not pass his notice that she asked a question about asking questions, and he fought to keep the smile from his face. "Those are my brothers." He tended to keep his answers simple, finding it so much easier than trying to explain. The truth was they were not his blood brothers. Cas had been an only child, fate dealing him a blow when he was placed into the foster care system at the age of eleven.

Two of his earlier foster homes had been temporary, families that only took children in emergencies, each stay lasting less than two months. Another one ended when the foster family discovered they were having a baby and no longer wanted to foster. The next had ended when the family decided to move out of the area.

By the time he landed with Miss Ethel, he was not sure he would ever have a lasting home. The seven other teenage boys were also under her care, creating a large family.

"I don't have any brothers or sisters," Bianca said, sighing. "I wish I did. It would be so much more fun. I would always have someone to play with. Someone to share secrets with. Someone to be with when I'm lonely."

Another rousing cacophony of cheers rose from the back yard, and her brows raised in surprise again. "How many brothers do you have?"

Shrugging, he said, “Seven.”

“Seven!” She suddenly burst out laughing, still bouncing on her toes. “That’s like living with the seven dwarfs!”

Rolling his eyes, he thought that if she could see the size of his brothers, the word dwarf would be the last description she would use. Before he had a chance to reply, a man stepped out onto the front porch of the house across the street and called, “Bianca! Time to come in!”

She waved toward the man before turning back to Cas. “That’s my dad. I have to go now. It was nice to meet you. I hope I can see you again.”

Her dad went back inside their house, and she darted toward the curb. Instinct took over, and Cas called out a warning. “Be careful! Look both ways first.”

She looked over her shoulder and gave him a brilliant smile as though his words had taken her by surprise and pleased her. Then he watched her trot across the street, telling himself that he just wanted to make sure she made it home safely. As soon as she disappeared inside, he turned and walked toward the front of his house.

Miss Ethel stepped onto the porch, her smile resting on him before it moved beyond his shoulder to the house across the street. “I believe we have new neighbors.”

Nodding, he said, “Yes, ma’am.”

“Was that their young girl you were speaking to?”

Nodding again, he said, “I was sitting under the trees when she came to the fence.” He chuckled. “When she found out I had seven brothers, she said it must be like living with the seven dwarfs. I didn't tell her how big they really were."

Miss Ethel laughed, placing her hand on his shoulder as they walked inside the house. "Well, I love a child with an imagination. She should be a sweet addition to the neighborhood."

She headed down the hall toward the back door to call his brothers in for dinner, and he turned and stared out the front porch screen door. The house across the street was smaller, but if it was just the girl and her father, they would not need as much room. He thought of the way her smile brightened her whole face and wondered if he would see much of her.

As he heard the noise of his brothers coming in from the back yard, he could not help but grin at her description. *Seven giants would be more like it.*

The oldest, Zander, was already over six feet tall. Rafe was about the same size as Zander, but Cael was already almost four inches taller than the twins, Jaxon and Jayden, who were in ninth grade, both coming close to six feet in height. That left the three youngest: Cas, Asher, and Zeke. All three in eighth grade, none of them were that tall yet, but Miss Ethel kept swearing that they would soon all need new clothes and shoes.

With a final glance across the street, he closed the door. She had been a cute kid to chat with, but a young girl had no business hanging around eight big boys, and he felt certain that her father would warn her away. Strange, but that thought brought him no peace.

"You seemed lost in thought today as you sat under the trees," Miss Ethel said softly.

It was nighttime and as was their custom every evening after reading, Miss Ethel would move to each boy and talk for a moment. It was a habit born from the time they came to live with her, and, as far as Cas knew, she had never broken the tradition.

They no longer read stories together, but each would spend time in the evenings reading. Television had its place in their lives, but she insisted the time before bed was best spent among the pages of a book.

Shrugging, Cas replied, "The trees remind me of my parents."

Nodding, a sad smile about her lips, she said, "I thought so. I'll bet you are so like your father. Tell me about him."

It was not the first time she had asked for stories about his family. Eyes lifted, he hesitated, pulling his thoughts together. "Dad liked to walk in the woods. He would place his hands on the bark of a tree and said he could feel the life underneath his fingertips. Even if there was a fallen log, he would show me the creatures that would live in the rotten wood. He'd say that trees were alive even when they were lying on the ground."

"What a fascinating man," she replied, her voice sincere. "And he taught you so much."

They were quiet for a moment and a small sigh slipped from his lips. Glancing to the side to assure that Zeke and Asher were still concentrating on the books they were reading, he whispered, "Sometimes, I'm afraid I'll forget."

"Forget what, Cas?"

He thought about his answer for a moment, memories sliding over him. "Forget my mom's cookies. Or the way my dad's hands were always rough from his work. Or the way the house smelled at Christmastime."

"Oh, no, my dear. You will always remember your parents. They will always be with you."

He looked up, doubt clouding his eyes, and she said, "To live in hearts we leave behind is not to die." She smiled. "A little quote by Thomas Campbell. Just like with my George, he lives in my heart, and your parents live in yours."

She kissed his forehead and moved off his bed, smiling as she left the room. As he closed his eyes he wondered about Bianca. *Had she lost her mom? And if so, did she remember her?*

2

The rain clouds that had gathered Friday night opened up and poured Saturday morning. Bianca sat at the table, her legs swinging underneath her chair, eating a bowl of cereal. Hoping to spend some time with her dad exploring their new side of the city, her eyes lit when he walked into the kitchen. Then her shoulders drooped when she took in his apparel.

"Dad! You're going to work on a Saturday?"

He walked over and gently tousled her hair. Not an overly tall man, he was very fit, and she thought he looked quite handsome in his suit. She was only six when her mother died, but she still remembered her mom smiling at him, saying he was the most handsome man she had ever met. Her dad had always laughed, kissed her mom, and said, "You're the most beautiful of all women." Then they would both look over at Bianca and say together, "Except for Bianca. She's the prettiest of all."

She hung onto those memories, young enough for

them to still make her heart ache and old enough to know that memories eventually fade.

"I'm sorry, Princess. I just need to go into work for a few hours this morning to make sure everything is straight in the office on Monday morning."

"Ugh!" She groaned and flopped back in her seat.

He fixed his cup of coffee, put it in a travel mug, then bent to kiss her forehead. Seeing the rain outside, he moved to get his overcoat and called out, "What are you doing today?"

She thought for a moment. "I'll go across the street and see if anyone wants to play with me."

Nodding, her father said, "That sounds fine, Princess. Just be safe."

Watching her father leave, she thought of Cas. She had liked discovering him as he sat under the tree, whittling. She had never met another boy that liked to carve wood and wished that they had been deep in the forest, not just under a tree in the neighborhood. *Maybe he would be a woodcutter. Or perhaps he was a prince in disguise. Or maybe an evil Queen sent him into the woods to look for innocent girls.* Grinning widely, she quickly rinsed her spoon and bowl and raced upstairs to get dressed. *Maybe I'll get to meet his seven little brothers today!*

All of Miss Ethel's boys sat at the breakfast table grumbling. They had games scheduled with Parks and Recreation for that morning, but with the forecast calling for rain, the games had been canceled.

"A rainy Saturday. Now what are we going to do?" Jaxon asked, slumping in his seat.

Zander sighed heavily. "I've got a big test coming up this week. I guess I can go ahead and study today to get a head start."

"Well, I've got quite a few inside chores that will keep us busy," Miss Ethel said, bringing another platter of eggs and bacon to the table.

Cas looked up. "Is there anything you need help with?"

Smiling, she said, "I need to go through some of your clothes to make a list of what can be handed down, what needs to be given away, and what new things need to be bought."

"We can all help with that." Cael grinned, adding, "If I keep growing, I'm gonna need everything new."

The doorbell rang, and Cas glanced toward Miss Ethel, seeing surprise on her face. Since the visitor did not seem to be expected, he offered, "I'll get it, Miss Ethel."

She nodded her thanks and continued planning some of the chores for the day with his brothers. Scooting his chair back, he walked down the hall from the dining room, past the large, informal living room, to the front door. Throwing it open, his mouth dropped open at the sight of Bianca standing on the porch.

She was wearing blue leggings and a bright yellow raincoat. Water dripped off the raincoat, creating a puddle by her flip-flop covered feet on the front porch. Her hood was pushed back, and her damp, black hair clung to her head, more water drops sliding down her widely smiling face.

Stunned, he startled when she lifted a hand, pushed her wet hair away from her eyes, and greeted, "Cas! Do you want to come and play?"

Feeling a presence behind him, he looked over his shoulder and saw Miss Ethel approaching, her eyes wide as she saw who was standing at the door.

"My goodness, you're soaking wet! Does your father know where you are?" Miss Ethel asked.

Shrugging, she said, "My dad's at work today, but he said it's okay if I play in the neighborhood."

Moving past Cas, Miss Ethel said, "Well, come in, come in. Let's get you dry."

Bianca walked in, smiled up at Cas, then her gaze moved behind Miss Ethel. He turned and watched his brothers walking down the hall toward them, curiosity on their faces. He could only imagine what a sight they made for a young girl, and he whipped his head around toward her again.

Her blue eyes bugged. "Wow! Are those your brothers?"

Nodding, he said, "Yeah. Uh… not really dwarfs, are they?"

Miss Ethel laughed, placed her hand on Bianca's shoulder, and drew her into the hall. Looking up, she said, "Zander, please get me a towel."

Zander darted into the small powder room and came back with a thick towel. Miss Ethel took it in her hands and gently rubbed it over Bianca's hair and face. "My dear, you have a hood on your raincoat.

Why did you not have it pulled up to cover your head?"

"You can't feel the rain on your face if your hood is blocking everything." Bianca smiled widely as she tilted her head back and stared up at them.

"Why did you want the rain on your face?" Jayden asked, his brow lowered.

Not wanting Bianca to feel embarrassed, Cas threw a glare toward Jayden and wondered how much trouble he would be in if he told his brother to shut up.

Bianca laughed, and Cas liked the sound. It was real… bubbling up from deep inside of her, not like the silly giggles from most of the girls in his class.

"I was running through the yard, pretending to be running through a forest with an evil goblin after me," Bianca said, still smiling. Suddenly, her brow scrunched. "I suppose that a princess running through a forest might have a cape with a hood on it, but if you have a goblin chasing you, you wouldn't take the time to pull it up." Seeming to have made up her mind, she smiled again and declared, "No, definitely running through the forest with the rain on your face would be the way to go."

Looking down at her, Cas blinked in surprise. He was also equally surprised that his brothers had nothing to say either.

"Well, that's certainly adventurous," Miss Ethel said, her eyes twinkling after having dried Bianca's hair. She stood and moved to the door, staring across the street before turning back to Bianca. "Are you sure your father doesn't mind you being over here today?"

Bianca nodded and poked her chest with her thumb. "I'm eleven. I know I'm small, but I'm not young. According to the American Red Cross Babysitting Course, I'm old enough to officially babysit someone else. Of course, they do mention how the maturity level of most eleven-year-olds can vary greatly, but I'm very mature."

She glanced down at her wet feet, then scrunched her nose. "I don't want to make a mess on your floor. I just wanted to know if Cas wanted to come out and play with me."

Heat infused his face and rushed through his body as well. He could only imagine what his older brothers would say at her request. Expecting instant teasing, he tightened his jaw.

Before they had a chance to say anything, she piped up, "But I can play with all of you. I thought you might be Cas' little brothers, like the seven dwarfs, but instead, you're more like the seven giants."

When no words or laughter came forth, he chanced a look over his shoulder, seeing the others staring slack-jawed and wide-eyed at their visitor.

Miss Ethel stepped forward, her hand once again on Bianca's shoulder. "Let me call your father and tell him that you're here. We had some chores we're going to take care of today, and you're more than welcome to stay with us until he gets home." Bianca quickly rattled off her father's name and phone number, and Miss Ethel moved into the kitchen to place her call.

Cas smiled at how a slip of a girl managed to stun and silence his brothers, something heretofore he had only seen when Miss Ethel spoke or lifted her brow in a silent message.

There was no fear in Bianca's face, but she sidled closer to him. Instead of irritation, a strange sense of protectiveness now settled over him. "These are my brothers, otherwise known as the dwarfs. Zander, Rafe, Cael, Jaxon, Jayden, Asher, and Zeke."

She beamed as she stepped closer. "Cool names. It's nice to meet you."

The others grinned, murmuring their greetings in return. Miss Ethel walked back down the hall and clapped her hands. "I talked to your dad, and he said it's fine for you to be here today."

"Great! What are you guys going to do?" Bianca asked.

"I've got the boys going through their clothes today, something you can't help with. But I'll also be doing some housework today."

Pulling off her rain slicker, Bianca looked around. "I'm great with housework. My dad says I'm a super organizer."

Soon, the house was abuzz with everyone working. While the eight boys went through their closets and drawers, carefully deciding which clothes could be handed down and which items needed to go into the giveaway pile, Bianca was scooting around the first floor, dusting and sweeping.

Eventually, Cas came down the stairs and found Bianca sitting in the living room, dusting all the books in the bookcases, humming to herself. Miss Ethel came around the corner, and he caught her eye. He mumbled, "I was just checking on her."

"Curious child," Miss Ethel said with a smile as she looked at Bianca. "She appears to be perfectly happy to help out." She turned her attention to him, her expression thoughtful. "You seem taken with her."

Shrugging, he said, "Nah. I just kinda feel like I found her… or rather, she found me. Guess I feel sorta responsible." He knew the truth was that there was something about Bianca that captivated him, but at thirteen years old, he was not about to admit to that.

"I'm going to start lunch. Why don't you ask her if she'd like to stay?"

As Miss Ethel disappeared down the hall again, he walked into the living room. Bianca, sitting cross-legged on the floor, had a stack of books next to her, and she was wiping each one carefully with a soft cloth. She looked up and grinned.

"You all have so many books. I love to read. Dad lets me go to the library but says we don't have enough room to keep many books. So, once I read them, I have to take them back." She looked down at the one in her hands. "I love the cover on this one. I wonder if your mom would let me borrow it or maybe just read it here when I come to visit."

He walked over and ran his finger along the spines of some of their favorites, looking at the book in her hands. The cover showed a watercolor painting of a quaint village. Maeve Binchy's Echoes. He smiled as his gaze drifted over some of the other books. "I was surprised the first time I came here and saw all of these.

Miss Ethel believes that everybody should read as much as they can."

Scrunching her nose, she asked, "Why do you call her Miss Ethel? Isn't she your mom?"

Taking a deep breath, he let it out slowly, his eyes darting to the side. "No, she's our foster mom." Seeing the confused look on Bianca's face, he said, "None of us have our real parents, so she takes us in and becomes our mom."

"You don't have a real mom either?" Her eyes were wide as she kept them pinned on him.

He was saved from answering when Miss Ethel called them to lunch. Bianca bounded to her feet, skipping down the hall as though it was an everyday occurrence for her to have lunch with them. Unable to keep the grin from his face, Cas followed.

"You can sit next to me," he said, sliding into one of the chairs. His brothers soon followed, all expressing gratitude over the platters of sandwiches and bowls of potato salad, coleslaw, and fruit. They waited until Miss Ethel had sat, said their prayer of thanks, and nodded before they began filling their plates.

Turning to Bianca, Cas asked, "Tell me what you want and I'll get it for you."

"I like it all!" she said, her eyes bright.

The gathering soon settled into eating, their conversation light and jokes abounding. Bianca seemed completely at ease with the large group, chattering happily.

"I was hoping for a girl my own age to live nearby

when we first moved in," she announced. "But this is even better."

Protectiveness once more surged within him, but he should not have been worried. His brothers appeared bemused by her, answering her many questions and listening as she talked incessantly.

"So, if you thought we were going to be the seven dwarfs, who is Cas?" Jaxon asked, his grin wide with a twinkle in his eyes. "The prince?"

Scrunching her nose, she shook her head. "No, I think the prince is kind of stupid." Her cheeks blushed bright pink as she turned to look at Miss Ethel. "I'm sorry. I know stupid isn't a nice word."

Miss Ethel smiled indulgently. "While it's true I don't usually condone name-calling, I'm more interested in why you're not impressed with the prince."

"Yeah, I thought all girls like the idea of the handsome prince," Rafe said, flexing his muscles and puffing out his chest in a mock pose.

"Have you *really* read the story of Snow White?" Bianca asked, looking around the table.

"Uh, yeah," came the responses from everyone in unison.

"We always read books and discussed them when we were younger," Zander claimed, his hard stare pinned on the younger girl.

"Actually, we still do," Zeke said, then shook his head slightly as he amended, "Well, not really fairy tales anymore."

Cael added, "Mr. Paulson, our sophomore English teacher, has us study a unit on fairy tales."

She lifted her small arms, palms upward, and said, "Then you get it. The prince in Snow White doesn't do *anything* special."

Cas shifted in his seat so that he could observe her animated face better as she spoke, ducking as her arms waved about, capturing everyone's attention.

"He doesn't even know about her," Bianca continued. "He isn't looking for her, searching for her, determined to find his true love. It's the dwarfs that love her. They're the ones that put her in the glass coffin. The prince does nothing more but wander through the woods and stumble upon her."

"I never thought of it that way," Asher mumbled, his soft voice sounding out as everyone sat in stunned silence.

"He just has his servants pick up the coffin that the dwarfs sweetly placed her in and carries her away. When one of his servants trips, it dislodges the piece of poisoned apple stuck in her throat. Talk about dumb luck! *Then* the prince kisses her. Jeez!" Flopping back in her chair, she puffed her bangs away from her forehead. "I mean, big deal! Everything he did just kinda happened."

Almost in unison again, the boys turned and looked at Miss Ethel, who was smiling widely. "My dear, that is incredibly insightful." Tilting her head to the side, she asked, "Where did you learn so much?"

Cas watched as a shadow passed across Bianca's face. With less animation, she replied, "My mom used to read to me all the time. When I was four years old, I could already read simple books. When I was five, I was already reading chapter books. My dad traveled a lot, so it was often just me and Mom."

The gathering was quiet, and Cas felt a pang in his heart as he knew what Bianca was going to say next. What they all knew she was going to say next. After all, loss instinctively understands loss.

With her thin shoulders lifting in a shrug, Bianca said, "My mom died when I was six. Dad works for my grandfather and took a new position so that he wouldn't travel as much. We moved out of our house… he said it made him sad to think of being there without Mom. For a while, we lived in an apartment, but he finally decided that I needed a house and a real neighborhood to live in. He still works a lot, but at least he's home at night."

Cas wanted to reach out and take her hand. He wanted to give her a hug and tell her that he knew the pain would never go away but that she would learn to live with it. Instead, he clenched his hands together in his lap, fighting the urge to comfort.

Her voice warm and soft, Miss Ethel said, "I'm so sorry for your loss, my dear. And while you can see that my boys are not dwarfs, you can visit us anytime you want. Although, I'm sure there are some girls in the neighborhood for you to play with."

Her nose scrunched again, and she shook her head, her silky, black hair swinging back and forth. "Oh, I don't mind that you have boys instead of girls! I don't even mind that they're giants instead of dwarfs!"

Suddenly blurting, Cas asked, "If I'm not the prince,

then who am I?" As soon as the words left his mouth, he wished he could pull them back in.

She turned to stare at him and her eyes brightened. Her smile lit her face and she declared, "You're like the huntsman. To me, he's the true hero in the story. He was ordered to kill Snow White. The Queen commanded that he carve out her heart! But deep inside, he was a protector. He has a kind heart and couldn't do it. He saved Snow White's life and shielded her. If I had someone to fall in love with, it would be the huntsman. Someone who would actually shield me."

Seemingly oblivious to the surprised expressions on everyone's faces, Bianca took the last bite of her lunch, settled back in her chair, and patted her still-flat belly.

"Well, I declare," Miss Ethel said. "I never thought about that particular aspect of the story. It just goes to show that you can always learn something new."

"That's weird," Asher said, shaking his head. When Bianca turned her face toward him, he explained. "Cas' name means *shield*."

She twisted around and smiled at Cas, reaching out to touch his arm. "I knew your name was cool!"

With the meal finished, he started to gather the plates since it was his turn to wash dishes. Bianca jumped up to help him. As he left the room, he heard Zander say, "Looks like Cas has a little assistant."

Jayden added, "He's lucky. I never get a helper when it's my turn to wash."

Ignoring his brothers, he led Bianca into the kitchen, and side-by-side they washed the plates from lunch.

"My, my, you are a little helper," Miss Ethel declared,

her smile warm as she walked over and gave Bianca a hug. "You can certainly come over anytime as long as your father says that it's okay."

Bianca smiled in return. "I'd like that. You have a nice family, Miss Ethel."

"Thank you, Bianca." She looked at the young girl and tilted her head slightly, "You have an interesting name. Not very common."

Cas watched as Bianca nodded seriously. "My mom told me that it's Italian. It means white. I was born in the middle of a snowstorm, and Mom used to tell me that Dad almost didn't get her to the hospital in time."

"Well, we're certainly glad he did, Miss Bianca Winters." With a pat on the little girl's shoulder, Miss Ethel started to turn and walk out of the room, a smile curving her lips. She stopped suddenly and glanced over her shoulder. "And, my dear, you may certainly borrow any books that you would like to read."

Bianca's eyes and smile widened, her face radiating joy. Later, as Cas walked her down the front walk to make sure she crossed the street safely, he noticed the book *Echoes* was tucked safely under her arm.

3

ONE YEAR LATER

Cas had been waiting for Bianca to come over, noticing that she had been very quiet on the school bus earlier. He could not imagine that anyone had been teasing her because just as quickly as she had wormed her way into their hearts, he and all his brothers made sure to let everyone know she had their protection.

On the verge of adolescence, she was even prettier but did not seem to realize it. She wore no makeup and her clothes consisted of jeans and t-shirts. Unlike other girls her age, she spent so much time living in her head, always thinking of stories and characters. Outgoing and friendly, everyone seemed to like Bianca, but he knew how mean teen girls could be. The light which normally beamed bright from her eyes seemed dimmer today. And when they got off the school bus, she tossed a small wave his way before going inside her house.

Unwilling to wait any longer, he jogged across the street and knocked on her door. She answered, and he noted her smile did not quite reach her eyes. Stepping inside, he had barely cleared the door when she threw herself into his arms. He held her close, then felt her body shake with what he thought was a sob.

Uncertain what to do, he simply continued to hold her. Finally, after a few minutes, she let go of him, wiped her cheeks, and said, "Thanks, Cas. I needed that."

"What's going on? Did somebody do something to you?" His hands were on her shoulders, and he fought the desire to curl them into fists at the idea that someone had hurt her.

Shaking her head, the movement caused her sleek hair to swing back and forth, the black tresses catching the light coming from the hallway. "No, no one hurt me. Nothing like that. It's just I felt very sad today, and there was something that I wanted to do, but my dad is working late and so we can't do it."

"Do what?" he asked, bending slightly to peer into her eyes. Bianca was so easy to get along with, he could not imagine there being something that she had wanted to do that the denial of it would cause such a reaction.

Unusually reticent, she finally said, "I wanted to go to the cemetery. Today would have been my mom's birthday. Dad always takes me on the anniversary of the day she died, but I don't like that. I'd rather go and celebrate her birthday with her."

"Do you know where it is?"

Her face fell as she shook her head. "I know it's the Richmond Memorial Cemetery, but I don't know the directions."

He sucked in a quick intake of air through his nose,

recognition spearing through him as pain shot through Cas' heart. Seeing her face and hearing her words, he would have given her anything... gladly. Zander was a senior and could drive. Cael and Rafe were juniors and also had their driver's licenses, but none of them could have a group of underaged passengers. That left Miss Ethel. Knowing what her answer would be, he grabbed Bianca's hand and said, "I know where it is. Let's go."

He checked to make sure she had her key and the door was locked behind them, and with her hand still in his, they ran across the street.

Just like he knew she would, Miss Ethel agreed immediately. Letting the other boys know what they were doing, Cas caught their expressions of sympathy, and his heart swelled as each of them gave her a hug.

Twenty minutes later, Miss Ethel sat in the big, old van that she used for shuttling the boys around while Cas walked with Bianca as she headed straight to a headstone. He was familiar with this cemetery but tried to force his thoughts to stay on Bianca and not his own memories.

Once in front of the headstone, Bianca pulled off her jacket, laid it on the ground, and sat cross-legged. Uncertain what to do, Cas stood awkwardly nearby until she looked over her shoulder, gave him a little smile, and patted the jacket next to her. Taking her silent invitation, he sat down next to her.

"I just wanted to come and say Happy Birthday, Mom. I'm getting better at baking, and I could've made you a cake today if you were still with us."

Cas sat quietly, listening as Bianca continued to chat

with her mom as though they were sitting at the table at home instead of in a cemetery where Cas was not sure her mom could hear her. It seemed to give Bianca a great deal of peace, so he remained still so as not to disturb her.

After a few minutes of chatting, Bianca leaned forward on her knees and placed a kiss on the cold granite headstone. Uncertain if she was going to burst into tears again, he breathed easier when she sat back down, turned her head up to him, and smiled.

Reaching over, she squeezed his hand and said, "You have no idea how much this means to me. I know I can talk to Mom anytime I want, but sometimes it's nice to sit here and do it."

He had intended to remain quietly supportive, but words blurted up from deep inside of him. "My parents are buried in this cemetery, too." As soon as he spoke, he snapped his lips shut and looked away. Besides the first time he had mentioned to Bianca that Miss Ethel was his foster mom, they had never talked about his real parents. It was unusual for a young girl to not be overly curious, but Bianca had simply told him one day that she would listen if he ever wanted to talk.

He felt tears hit the back of his eyes, and he blinked several times to keep them from falling. Part of him wished he could pull the words back in, and another part of him was glad that Bianca knew.

Her small hand in his gave another little squeeze, and she asked, "What happened?"

Sucking in a deep breath, he let it out slowly before he finally spoke. "They were on their way home from work and stopped at a convenience store to get some milk for the next day. They didn't realize the store was being robbed, and when they walked in, they startled the two men that had guns. They were both shot."

Her hand flinched, and he felt the pressure. She slowly eased her grip and gently rubbed her thumb over the back of his hand. "I didn't have any living relatives, so I was put into foster care. I was in a couple of them, but they weren't so great. Then I ended up with Miss Ethel, and she became my new mom."

"I'm sorry you don't have your real parents, but... if you have to be without them, I'm glad that you have Miss Ethel."

He liked her words, and they moved through him, slowly soothing. He liked that she did not pepper him with questions or make him feel weird. He turned toward her, seeing understanding in her blue eyes. "One of the policemen told me that my dad threw himself in front of my mom, trying to shield her. They both died anyway, but I like to think that the last thing my mom thought was that my dad tried to save her."

"Her shield. Oh, Cas, I love that. He was her shield."

A breeze began to blow, and he noticed Bianca's hair flowed back behind her as the sun made her blue eyes sparkle even more. It dawned on him that her father had brown hair, and he asked, "Do you look like your mother?"

Nodding emphatically, she brightened. "Yes! My father tells me that all the time, and when I look at pictures, I'm stunned because I look just like her."

"Then she must've been beautiful," he said, this time being the one to give her hand a little squeeze.

She bit her lip and smiled, then stood and pulled him up as well. She glanced toward the van where Miss Ethel sat before looking back up at Cas. "Can we go to your parents? Would that be okay?"

Knowing Miss Ethel would not mind at all, he agreed. They began to walk to a different section of the cemetery, finally stopping at a wide, double, granite headstone. He had never sat at his parents' resting place and was uncertain what Bianca would do. They stood side-by-side for a moment, then she bent toward the headstone and whispered, "I really like your son. You'd be so proud of Cas. He's a super nice boy." Standing, she moved back, linked fingers with him, and lifted her face to the sun.

Turning back to him, she asked, "Do you think they look down on us? You know… from Heaven? Maybe keep an eye on us or just watch us? Maybe like angels… only not the kind with wings? Or maybe like the stars?"

Before he had a chance to consider his words, he said, "Silently, one by one, in the infinite meadows of heaven, Blossomed the lovely stars, the forget-me-nots of the angels."

She sucked in a gasp, and her eyes brightened with unshed tears. Then she spoke with a barely heard whisper. "That's beautiful. I know that one. It's from Henry Wadsworth Longfellow. I love his poems."

He held her gaze, surprised she had not laughed at him. She was always surprising him. "Sometimes I write poetry as well. It's not good—"

"I want to read it." She spoke quickly, her eyes still blinking back tears. Her gaze remained pinned on him, penetrating deep inside. She squeezed his hand and said, "I think anything you write would be good because it came from you."

He slowly reached into his pocket and pulled out a piece of paper, handing it to her with trembling hands. He had never shared any of his poems, and fear snaked through him now, wondering if she would think it was ridiculous.

She took the paper from him and pressed it to her chest reverently before unfolding it, careful of the well-worn creases. Immediately she read aloud. *"Been fishing in the river of sorrow, hunting for today but catching tomorrow, Any disposition makes me vulnerable, looking at my reflection, I feel other than honorable, I only seek to find but I'm left behind, Just as I catch up it's like I press rewind, So I will keep searching for today as tomorrow is hollow, And release my fear of the unknown so my future can follow."*

Her voice had quivered as she finished the poem, her hands shaking. She peered deeply into his eyes and said, "Oh, God, Cas… this is the most beautiful thing I have ever read." He had started to shrug, but she shook her head, sending her hair swinging about her shoulders. "No, really! Your words are so beautiful. They make me feel… really feel."

His shoulders relaxed as she handed the paper back to him. Once it was tucked safely away in his pocket, she reached down and grabbed his hand, leaning her head against his shoulder as they stood quietly.

After several minutes, he glanced over the top of her head toward the van. "We need to head back. Come on."

She grinned and did not let go of his hand as they walked to where Miss Ethel was waiting. A warm breeze continued to blow, and he was filled with peace.

4

ONE YEAR LATER

Bianca jogged across the road toward Miss Ethel's house under the watchful eye of Cas. He unsuccessfully tried to ignore the way her body had matured. Even though she was still petite, it was impossible to not notice her breasts bouncing slightly as she ran. Her arms were full of more books she was returning. She had once declared that Miss Ethel's house was as good as any library, and she was determined to read all she could.

When she arrived at the fence, her eyes met his and she laughed. "I'm thirteen, Cas. I think I can be trusted to cross the street without you watching after me."

With his hands on his hips, he shook his head. "Bianca, you daydream so much, I'm afraid you'll step right in front of a bus while your mind is on the story you're creating in your head."

She rolled her eyes and playfully punched him on the shoulder. They were not standing at the front gate but near the trees. At fifteen, he had grown quite a bit since she first met him, and considering he worked out with his brothers, his body was developing hardened muscles. He reached across the fence, and with one hand on her back and the other hand scooping from behind her knees, he plucked her into the air, easily lifting her over the fence.

They walked to the blanket he had spread out and sat together. She looked down at her hands and sighed softly. "I've got some news."

He looked over at her, unable to discern from her tone of voice if the news was good or bad. Her nose was scrunched, but other than that, she gave no outward clues. "What's up?"

She plucked a nearby blade of grass and fiddled with it for a moment before finally admitting, "My dad is getting married."

Cas blinked, her words surprising him. "Married?"

She nodded slowly, a crinkle still on her brow. "Yeah. I mean, he's been dating her for a while, but I didn't know they were considering marriage. You've seen her a couple of times. Her name's Lucille. She's pretty… in a fancy sort of way. She always makes sure to tell people that she was Miss Harrison County when she graduated from high school." A giggle slipped out as she added, "That's not exactly Miss Universe!"

Cas smiled and shoulder bumped her. "Wow, a beauty queen for a stepmother."

"Well, it beats an evil queen, that's for sure!"

They both laughed, and as always, he liked the sound of her laughter. "Do you like her?" he asked, expecting a simple yes or no, but she appeared to give great thought to his question.

Nibbling on her bottom lip, she finally shrugged. "When they first started going out, she made a big deal about me. She'd talk about how nice it would be to have a girl to teach how to fix hair and wear makeup. How nice to have a girl to take shopping. But lately, I get the feeling that she doesn't like sharing the attention that Dad gives me."

"Maybe she's just more used to having you around, so she doesn't have to talk about it so much."

Shaking her head, she said, "She's starting to complain."

"About what?"

"For one, I don't think she likes this neighborhood."

Jerking back, he repeated, "Doesn't like this neighborhood?"

"Yeah, she says we should live in a bigger house." She gave her head a little shake as though to clear her thoughts and blew out her breath. "Ugh. I don't want to think about her anymore." Looking down at the pieces of wood nearby, she asked, "What are you working on?"

He picked up the wood and rubbed his thumb over the impressions he had been carving. "I'm trying to carve the Army emblem for Zander. It's a lot more intricate than what I've done before, and this is about my fifth attempt."

She took the palm-sized, flat, circular wood and studied the intricate carvings of flags, canons, and cannonballs. Her eyes were wide as she turned her head and looked up at him. "This is amazing. Zander's going to love it."

His stoic oldest brother had graduated from high school last spring and joined the Army. While they were all proud of him, getting used to missing the first of them to leave home was hard. Snorting, he said, "You know Zander. He'll look at it, thank me, then probably throw it in a drawer."

She huffed and retorted, "I do know Zander. He'll look at it, thank you, and then promptly hang it on his wall!"

He could not deny that she did know Zander. In the last two years since that day she had popped over to see if he would play before discovering he was a teenager with seven teenage brothers, she had become a constant figure at Miss Ethel's house.

She treated each of his brothers like her own, receiving their affection in return. Miss Ethel easily slid into the role of female mentor, something Bianca craved. She had even sat at Miss Ethel's feet and learned how to knit. She may have been younger than the rest of them, but she joined their lively discussions of literature, often challenging them to think in ways they had not.

Cas was never quite sure of his place in her world. From the moment she stated that she saw him as the huntsman instead of the prince, he felt the need to take on that role. He had met her dad numerous times but often felt that Mr. Winters was distracted, glad that his daughter had a safe place to hang out while he was at work. Her dad lavished love on Bianca but did not seem really invested in what she was doing.

Looking down at the carved wooden disc in his hand, he knew she was right. Zander would appreciate the effort and the results.

She sat with her legs bent, arms wrapped around her shins and her chin propped on top of her knobby knees. "It's not quite the same without him, is it?"

Shaking his head, he said, "No. I can tell the others miss him, and Miss Ethel is sad but says it was time for him to go out on his own."

"That's the way of life, though, isn't it? We live, we grow older, and we die. And if we're lucky, along the way we find love and friendship."

His gaze jumped to hers, blue eyes pinned to his. She was only in eighth grade but so unlike any of the girls he knew. Miss Ethel always said Bianca had an old soul. He was never quite sure what she meant by that, but right now, staring into Bianca's eyes after what she had just said, he understood. It was as though she had lived a thousand lifetimes in her thirteen years.

He thought back to when he shared more of his story of how he came to live with Miss Ethel. It was odd that Bianca, so inquisitive, would have let him tell the story when he was ready. It was after the initial tale he told her at the cemetery. It was on the anniversary of his parents' death, and she had found him sitting under the trees. As though she could tell his heart was heavy, she said nothing but sat with him. He once thought that loss recognized loss, and in that moment, he knew it was true.

He had shared everything he could remember about his parents, and it had felt so good to unburden his memories to her. And just like when he shared his poems, she leaned her head against his shoulder.

Now, the air hung heavy between them, and his gaze dropped to her mouth. She had been experimenting with a little makeup, and today her lips were slicked with gloss that was lightly tinged red, giving them a ruby glow.

He jerked his gaze away, knowing it was ridiculous to stare at her mouth. She was too young, and he refused to let his thoughts travel down the path that his teenage body always seemed to want to go. It was ridiculous that now that he was in high school he still had not met another girl that he cared for more than Bianca.

His thoughts were interrupted as a car drove slowly past, the sound of multiple giggles emanating from the open windows. It was not the first time a group of teenage girls had driven down to the end of the cul-de-sac where Miss Ethel lived, hoping to find some of the boys outside. While he did not think he was anything special to look at, he knew the girls were crazy for his brothers, especially Rafe and Jaxon, who enjoyed the attention.

"Hey, Cas!" several of the girls shouted as they spotted him in the yard.

He remained seated but threw his hand up in a slight wave, lifting his chin in silent acknowledgment.

"Oh, sorry, we didn't see you had someone with you. It's too bad you have to babysit today!" The sound of renewed giggles followed the insult, and he jumped to his feet. He sent them on their way with a glare, watching as the car turned the corner and drove out of sight.

Light fingertips touched his back, and he twisted his head, seeing Bianca standing behind him, staring up into his face. "I'm sorry, Bianca. Ignore them. They're just stupid girls."

She shrugged as she dropped her gaze, "I know. It only hurts if I let their arrows land on me." Her lips curved into a slow smile and she lifted her head to stare at him again, "You've always been my shield. When you're around, their arrows bounce off."

Her words caused his breath to leave in a rush at the idea that he had been her shield, even if it was only with words. Needing to move past the tangle of emotions that had begun to creep in when she was around, he rolled his eyes and said, "You want to stay for dinner?"

"When have I not wanted to stay for dinner?" She laughed, then glanced across the street at her house. "Dad will be out with Lucille, as usual."

Together they packed up his carvings and knives and walked toward the house.

A few days later, Bianca sat in her usual place on the floor of Miss Ethel's living room while the boys were all lounging around, doing their homework. Occasionally, one of them would work in their room or at the dining room table if they needed extra quiet or space, but often they stayed in the living room.

Cas, Zeke, and Asher were in tenth grade, all three having Mr. Paulson for sophomore literature. They were in different classes but had the same assignment, this time studying fairy tales.

Bianca did not have any homework to do, so she sat cross-legged, knitting. As was her habit, she often glanced up toward Cas, loving to watch him concentrate. If she were honest, she loved watching him do anything. She knew he considered her a friend, and for that she was glad. But to her young heart, she considered him to be so much more.

"This is crazy stuff," Cas huffed, looking up from his book.

Miss Ethel peered at him from over the rim of her glasses, her needles never ceasing in their movements. "Which fairy tale did you decide to write about in your paper?"

It was not lost on Bianca that he glanced her way before answering.

"Snow White."

Jayden laughed and looked down where she was sitting. "Bianca, do you remember when you thought we were the seven dwarfs?"

She smiled and nodded, although she felt the heat of a blush creep over her cheeks. Turning her attention back to Cas, she asked, "What crazy stuff are you reading?"

"Because of the Grimm brothers and the Disney movie, everybody is super familiar with the story of

Snow White," he began. "What I didn't know is that there are some inspirations that are based in real life."

Bianca glanced down, her lips now curving gently. "Margaretha von Waldeck?"

"What?" Jaxon and Jayden exclaimed in unison.

She looked up and saw the surprise on the other boys' faces, interest in Miss Ethel's eyes, and a slight smile from Cas as he nodded.

"I should've known you would know this," he laughed.

Shrugging, she said, "My mom and I would read stories, and when I got older, I would dig a little to find out where some of the stories came from." She giggled, "I know, I know. I'm weird!" As her mirth slowed, she kept her eyes on Cas. "Please, go on. Tell us what you're learning."

"Well, in the 1500s, Margaretha was a German countess who was forced to move to another country by her stepmother. But while she was there, she fell in love with a prince who would later become the King of Spain. Her father and stepmother disapproved of the relationship because it was politically inconvenient. Then she mysteriously died, apparently having been poisoned. Some historical accounts say that it was the prince's father, the King of Spain, who opposed the match and had her murdered."

"History is not always kind, nor easy to learn," Miss Ethel said. "I've always found it interesting that children's stories often came from these rather harsh tales."

Continuing, Cas said, "One study has come up with over fifty Snow White variances. In the first Grimm brothers' version, it was the biological mother that abandoned her. They say that it was probably later changed to a stepmother so that children would not be so frightened of the story. There's also an Albanian tale, and Malaysian, Indian, Armenian, and Russian versions. There's even a Roman legend that's similar, but it's pretty rough."

"And the moral of the story of Snow White?" Miss Ethel asked.

"Don't talk to strangers!" Zeke exclaimed, drawing nods from the others.

"Unless you can handle yourself," Jaxon quipped, striking a pose, showing off his biceps and earning a pillow tossed at him from Asher.

"Classically, I'd say it's that real beauty comes from within," Cas replied. "The evil queen was completely concerned with outward beauty but had a black soul."

"And it's good to have friends," Bianca piped up from her place on the floor, her smile wide. Her gaze moved across the brothers sitting around the room before landing on Cas. "I didn't move into a neighborhood with dwarfs, but I definitely gained friends!"

The others went back to their studying, Miss Ethel went back to her knitting, but Bianca held Cas' gaze for a long time, a warm understanding seeming to flow between them. She finally turned and leaned her back against the sofa and continued her knitting, feeling his leg pressed against her shoulder. And she smiled.

5

TEN MONTHS LATER

Cas stood to the side, watching Bianca tearfully hug Rafe and Cael. The next two of Miss Ethel's boys were ready to board the bus that would take them to boot camp. Joining Zander in the desire to enlist in the military after high school, they were making their rounds of goodbyes.

Their brothers had stepped up first, then Bianca rushed in, her arms encircling Rafe, accepting his embrace and kiss on the top of her head before she turned to Cael. Still petite at fourteen years old, she barely came to their chests.

Cas watched as she stepped back, wiped her cheeks, then hurried to his side where he wrapped his arm around her.

His brothers had saved Miss Ethel for last, and Cas watched as she offered a watery smile to her boys.

"I'm proud of you," she said. "Not because of the service you're getting ready to provide, but for who you are as men." She leaned in, and they bent to place their ears near her as she whispered.

Cas watched as they both grinned, their fingers tightening slightly as they hugged her thin frame to their tall, muscular bodies.

"I'll remember," both said in unison.

She reached up and gently patted their cheeks, reminding them of her love before stepping back and joining the younger boys and Bianca. Soon the bus rolled out of the station, and Miss Ethel handed the keys to the van over to Jayden, giving him permission to drive them home. When it looked like Jaxon was about to protest, she lifted her eyebrow and said, "When you are a little lighter on the accelerator, then you can drive me."

Jaxon grinned, well known for his *aw-shucks* expression that never worked on Miss Ethel but always made Cas laugh. Bianca caught his look and giggled as well.

Once home, Miss Ethel settled in her wingback chair in the living room and picked up her knitting needles. Bianca sat cross-legged on the floor, her back against Cas' legs, her own knitting basket next to her, and the two women's needles clicked, the sound comforting.

"Miss Ethel," Bianca began. "I know it was private, but can I ask what you whispered to Rafe and Cael before they left?"

The edge of Miss Ethel's lips quirked upward, "You know, I have often shared my love of literature with the boys and firmly believe in the power of the written word. I simply shared with them a quote from a very great author."

Cas stared at her, aware that Jaxon, Jayden, Asher, Zeke, and Bianca were perfectly still, waiting to hear what words of wisdom she had passed on to Cael and Rafe.

Looking up from her knitting, she sent her loving gaze about the room, moving over all of them before saying, "*You have brains in your head. You have feet in your shoes. You can steer yourself any direction you choose. You're on your own. And you know what you know. And YOU are the one who will decide where to go.* "

Bianca threw her head back and laughed. Her black hair cascaded in a silken sheet down her back, and her blue eyes sparkled as she turned and looked toward Cas before giving her attention back to Miss Ethel. "You quoted Dr. Seuss to them?"

The others joined in laughter as Miss Ethel smiled indulgently. "I've also taught my boys to not be literary snobs. We can find great words to live by in all sorts of places."

Bianca leaned against Cas' legs as her needles continued to click. Sitting in the living room, surrounded by four of his brothers, happy that three of his brothers were off doing what they wanted to do, the woman that had become his mother, and the girl that was his best friend, he knew that life could not get any better.

One Year Later

Bianca came back from Miss Ethel's house, a smile on her face and a plate of brownies in her hand. Lucille did not cook often and certainly never made sweets. "The last thing my figure needs is calories!" Lucille would say before spearing Bianca with a pointed look and clucking, "But then, with unfortunate looks like yours, the extra sweets can't hurt."

Sighing, she wished for the millionth time that her dad had not married Lucille. They had only been married for a few months, but it had not taken long for Bianca to see that Lucille had no desire to be a mother to her… at least not a kind mother.

Setting the plate of brownies on the kitchen counter, she wondered if she should hide them from Lucille for fear that her stepmother would throw them out. Hearing voices coming from the living room, she slipped off her shoes by the door — another rule of Lucille's — and padded toward the front of the house.

"Lionel, I'm working on Henry."

She halted, hearing the name of Lucille's much younger brother who lived in California. She grimaced at the memory of meeting him at the wedding. She had first thought him handsome, but the more time she had spent around him, her description had morphed into *smarmy*. Lucille had fawned over Lionel, and Bianca had watched as the young man sucked up to her dad. He had also tried to cozy up to her, but she hated the way his gaze moved over her body, resting on her breasts when no one else was around. *Ugh!*

"I hate living in this southern suburbian hell," Lucille continued, her phone pressed to her ear. "With the money Henry makes and what he has in the bank, we should be in a gated community... or at least in a large house with a pool. Yes... yes... I know..."

Bianca slid back toward the kitchen, not wanting Lucille to know that she had come in. She could not help but grin. Lucille was going to be disappointed. She knew her dad would not make her move while she was in high school. And now that she was in ninth grade, they would stay where they were. She thought of Cas and the years they had together before he graduated. Sitting in the kitchen, she took the plate of brownies and bit into one, loving the chewy, chocolatey goodness.

"Oh, you're home already." Lucille walked into the room. "I thought you'd be over at Old Ethel's house."

Jaw tight, Bianca hated the way Lucille called Miss Ethel the rude name of Old Ethel. "I was but came back to bring the brownies *Miss* Ethel made for us."

"Whatever," Lucille said, dismissively waving her hand about. She looked at the plate and lifted her nose into the air. "You might as well pig-out on them. Your dad and I are going to dinner."

Rolling her eyes, she mumbled, "What else is new?" A sarcastic smile slid over her face as she looked up at her stepmother. "It's strange that you go out to eat all the time. My mom used to cook the most wonderful meals all the time. Much healthier, you know."

A long red fingernail tapped on the counter next to

her. Lucille leaned down and held Bianca's gaze, a sneer on her mouth. "Don't get too comfortable here, my little *princess*. Your days of ruling your dad are soon going to be over, and I'll be the reigning one."

Before she had a chance to respond, Bianca's dad walked into the house. "Lucille, Bianca! How nice to see my two girls together."

Lucille narrowed her eyes at Bianca before turning and, with a huge smile on her face, cried out, "Henry! You're home early. And I've got to change for dinner. After all, I can't have you be seen with me not looking my best."

"Oh, my dear," he assured, "You're always beautiful."

As Lucille wandered down the hall, he bent to kiss the top of Bianca's head. "Hey, Princess. You ready to go out?"

Shaking her head, she lied, "I ate with Miss Ethel, so I'll stay home and do my homework."

"Well, okay, sweetheart, if you're sure." He gave her shoulders a squeeze, ruffled her hair, and wandered down the hall after Lucille.

Her eyes followed his retreat and she sighed loud and long. Closing her eyes, she cringed at the thought of three more years under the same roof as Lucille. *Maybe when all of Miss Ethel's boys have graduated she'll let me live with her!*

One Year Later

Cas stood underneath the copse of trees in the front corner of the yard, staring at the moving van across the street. In one week, he, along with the last two of Miss Ethel's full-time boys, Zeke and Asher, would be boarding the bus that would take them to their respective boot camps. He already had it firmly set in his mind how the goodbyes would go.

Miss Ethel would hug all three of them and, with tears in her eyes, whisper words of wisdom. Bianca would hug Zeke and Asher, telling them how much she was going to miss them. Then she would move into his arms, where he would finally tell her how much she meant to him. He would kiss her but not on the top of her head. After tilting her face up to his, he would take her lips in their first kiss. And then he would promise that he would come home to her.

He had imagined that scene so many times in the past weeks that it was as real to him as if it had already happened. But instead, she had come to their house yesterday, her eyes red and swollen with tears.

When he first saw her, he leapt to his feet, fists clenched, ready to take on whoever had hurt her. But between her sobs, he learned that her father was transferring, and they were moving across the country. It seemed Lucille had reached the end of her tether with living in suburbia and wanted to move to where her brother was in California. Her dad had not warned Bianca, giving in to Lucille's suggestion that they keep

Bianca in the dark until the last minute so as not to upset her.

And today, the moving van arrived, loaded their belongings, and had just pulled out into the road. It felt as though his heart was splitting in two. He lifted his hand and rubbed over his chest, trying to massage the ache deep inside.

He heard Miss Ethel's screen door slam shut, and he looked behind him to see Bianca leaving the house, wiping her cheeks. She had been inside, saying goodbye to Zeke, Asher, and Miss Ethel.

She looked up and saw him standing in the shade and hurried to him, her face crumpling once more. He opened his arms wide and enveloped her in a hug. They stood for a long moment, neither able to think of words that would fit the moment, the emotion overwhelming everything.

Finally, sucking in a deep breath, she said, "You just graduated from high school, and you're getting ready to leave. This is not how I thought we would say goodbye to each other." She leaned her head back and peered up at him, her gaze searching his face before she added, "Shakespeare was an idiot. Parting is *not* sweet sorrow. It's just plain sorrow."

Sliding his hands up to her cheeks, he tilted her head ever so slightly and bent to take her lips in the softest of kisses. He knew it was her first kiss, and while he wanted to take it deeper, he kept it light. Their tongues darted out, touching tentatively before he pulled back and pressed her cheek against his heartbeat.

"It doesn't matter that I'm going far away," she said.

"I laid in bed last night and realized that staying here without you while you left for the Army would have broken my heart. So, just think of it as us both going away at the same time."

Her father and stepmother came out of the house, locked it for the last time, and met the real estate agent on the sidewalk. They chatted for just a moment and then he turned the keys over to her. Looking across the street, her father called out, "Bianca! It's time for us to go."

"I'll never forget you," he said, bending to kiss her one last time.

"Nor will I forget you," she promised, leaning up on her tiptoes to accept his kiss.

As he regretfully forced his arms to let her go and watched her walk across the street one last time, he could not help but wonder when — or if — he would see her again.

6

TWELVE YEARS LATER

Bianca stepped out of the courthouse into the hot California sunlight, her heels clicking on the granite steps. Her sleek, black hair hung in a sheet that reached below her shoulders, gently blowing back in the small breeze. She slid her tailored jacket off her shoulders and draped it over her arm. Her classic navy straight skirt that reached just above her knees and pale blue silk shell blouse gave her an air of sophisticated confidence.

Standing on the top step, she pulled her sunglasses from her purse, gave them a flick, and slid them onto her face. She sucked in a deep breath, letting it out slowly, feeling the stress and anxiety from the past several years slowly leave her body.

Hoping to avoid another confrontation, she hurried down the steps of the courthouse and made her way to the parking lot at the side of the building. Approaching her small, old SUV, she heard her name called out and sighed heavily. *I should've known I couldn't just make a clean getaway.*

Turning, she watched as Lucille and her brother, Lionel, approach and prayed it was the last time she ever had to lay eyes on either one of them. Lucille, in her fifties, still dyed her hair solid black. Her clothing was expensive, and Bianca wondered how her step-mother would enjoy shopping for bargains. Of course, before that happened, she would probably marry again.

Lionel, only in his thirties, also had black hair, but his was still natural in color. It had always angered her when people assumed that Lucille was her mother and Lionel was her brother simply based on their hair color. It had also angered her that her father so often did not correct other people's assumptions. But she did. Every chance she got.

Neither Lucille nor Lionel had worked a day in their lives, and she wondered if that would also change soon.

"I don't think we have anything else to say to each other," she began as they neared. "The judge's decision is final. My father's will stands as it was written."

Lucille would be considered by many to be beautiful, but much of it was due to plastic surgery and a variety of monthly treatments received when she spent a day or so at the exclusive spa she was so fond of. But now, her mouth, slicked dark red with lipstick, twisted in an ugly sneer. "Your father never meant to cut us out. That was your doing!"

She turned her head slightly and looked at Lionel. He had cleaned up his appearance for court, but she knew his true colors. Often drunk or high. Always looking for an easy way to make money, seemingly unwilling to admit that hard work might be the key.

"My father would have given you much, but my mom's inheritance was never something you were going to get. But then, considering he had seen you waste your life, he wasn't about to offer you more."

Lucille's fingers curled and Bianca swallowed, determined not to show fear, having felt the sting of her stepmother's slap before. "Careful, Lucille. I've felt your claws and don't intend to feel them again. There's a police station directly behind us." She noted both their eyes dart to the building before shifting back to her.

Lionel stepped forward to place a hand on his sister, and Bianca assumed he was trying to calm Lucille. It was to no avail.

"Bianca, I gave your father my best years and helped take care of him when he was ill—"

"You walked all over him, wondering when he was going to die, assuming that you were going to get any money that came from my mother's family. I'm only glad that at the end he saw through you."

Lucille opened her mouth to retort, but Bianca was done. Completely and irrevocably done. Throwing her hand up, palm outward, she said, "Everything that needed to be said was said in court. The judge made his decision that Dad's will stands as written. I'm leaving here, and I never want to see either of you again."

She turned and hurried to her vehicle, climbing inside. She could hear Lucille continuing to call out threats, but she started the ignition and let the engine drown out the annoying voice. Driving away, she glanced at the rearview mirror, seeing both of them grow smaller in the distance.

Smiling for what seemed like the first time in years, she thought of Jack Kerouac's On the Road and quoted out loud, "What is that feeling when you're driving away from people and they recede on the plain till you see their specs disappearing? It's the too-huge world vaulting us, and it's goodbye. But we leaned forward to the next crazy adventure beneath the skies."

Continuing toward her small apartment, her plans already made and ready for executing, she grinned. *Now, it's my time for the next crazy adventure.* And she was sure her father would agree.

Bianca pulled into the small gas station. She climbed from her older model SUV, lifting her arms above her head in a back-cracking stretch. Once the gas tank was filled, she pulled into a parking space at the front and walked inside, pushing her sunglasses up onto the top of her head where they held her hair back from her face. After using the restroom, she glanced at the coffee station longingly but passed it by. Opting instead for water, she also grabbed some cheese crackers. Paying for her purchases, she glanced out the window, a little sigh leaving her lips.

"You been on the road long?"

She looked at the older man behind the cash register and smiled. His hair was white, patches of it standing out in odd directions. Nodding, she replied, "Yes. I've been on the road for thirteen days."

His bushy white eyebrows rose to his forehead and

he blew out his breath in a long whistle. "Thirteen days! You must be on a sightseeing drive!"

Twisting her long, straight black hair into a messy bun that she fastened with a clip, she said, "I decided it was time to make a change in my life. At the same time, I figured I might as well see some different parts of the country."

"Where did you start from?" He rested his weight on his forearms as he leaned onto the messy counter littered with packs of gum, candy bars, and an old dish filled with pennies next to the cash register. His attention was centered on her as though he had all the time in the world for a chat.

She glanced around at the empty store and realized that on this lonely stretch of country road, he probably did not get a lot of traffic. Especially someone whose vehicle had California license tags. "I've been living in California for a number of years but spent some of my youth in Virginia. I've wanted to come back for such a long time." Shrugging, she added, "And, since I was driving from the other side of the country, I decided to sightsee along the way."

"I ain't been out of Virginia," he said, then lifted his hand to rub over his scruffy beard. "Except for the year I spent in Nam, but that sure as hell wasn't sightseeing." He chuckled, then went into a coughing fit for a moment. He jerked his head toward the cigarettes lined up in neat rows in the display behind him. "Gave 'em up years ago, but they still stole part of my lungs."

Uncertain what to say to that, she simply nodded

and waited as he finished running her credit card transaction.

"What all did you see?" he asked when he finally gained control of himself.

"I drove up to Washington and then into Montana before heading south. I came through Wyoming and Colorado. I saw the Rocky Mountains and the Great Plains." She closed her eyes for a moment, the sights and sounds and smells of her trip moving back through her memory, and a little smile played about her lips. "I went south to Oklahoma and Texas, going all the way to Houston so that I could stand in the water of the Gulf of Mexico."

"Lordy be!" he exclaimed, and her eyes jumped open to see him still leaning forward, his eyes sparkling. "Where'd you go from there?"

"I cut through Louisiana and Mississippi, hit the corner of Alabama before coming into Tennessee. I kept going north so that I could come through the Smoky Mountains of East Tennessee and North Carolina. Made it into Virginia, and here I am."

"That sounds like a mighty fine trip to me." He beamed as he slid off a stool. She was surprised to discover he was very short and she was now looking down at him. He continued, "Sounds like you went to a lot of places and saw a lot of things."

Nodding, she could not help but meet his smile. "I did. It's been a good trip."

Cocking his head to the side, he stared up at her, and she felt his intense gaze peering deep inside before he lowered his voice. "Did you find what you were looking for?"

His question surprised her, causing her to hesitate. Pulling her lips between her teeth for a moment, she finally released them as she sighed and shook her head. "No. Not exactly… not yet." Swallowing deeply under his never-wavering perusal, she let out a long, slow breath. "But I'm hoping to."

"Do you know what you're hoping to find?"

Her tongue darted out to moisten her bottom lip. Somehow his probing questions did not feel intrusive. "I want to see if I can connect… to my past… if that's even possible."

"And where's your past?"

"Richmond… it's in Richmond. So, that's where I'm going."

His blue eyes continued to sparkle underneath his bushy white eyebrows. Staring at him, she thought he looked just like one of the characters from a fairy tale book her mother used to read from. With a mental shake, she pushed that thought to the side. *I must be truly tired.*

His gaze never wavered as he inclined his head toward the window overlooking the road. "You might want to stay off the interstate. I heard on the radio that there's a big wreck up ahead and it's got traffic backed up for miles and miles."

"Oh, no!" Her shoulders slumped. She had no end plan at moment other than to find a hotel for the next few evenings, at least until she discovered if her past still existed in the present. The last thing she wanted was to be stuck in traffic.

"You can stay on the back roads, though. There's lots of nice country roads around here. It'll give you a chance to see some scenery." Chuckling, he added, "Never know what you'll find along the road when you take a chance."

With that, he handed her credit card back to her. She placed it into her wallet, then hesitated before thanking him. She walked back out into the sunshine, lifting her face toward the sun for a moment. The air was clear, and she felt strangely lighter. After climbing into her vehicle, she pulled onto the road. In the last two weeks, she had seen mountains, plains, rivers, lakes, oceans, farmland, big cities, and small towns. She had seen places of great beauty, and in each one she had wondered if it was a place she could settle.

But her heart longed for something else, and she had learned to listen to that feeling inside. So, she continued her journey to the east. Perhaps toward the only place she had ever truly felt love and friendship.

Checking her GPS, she could see no evidence of traffic on the highways or mention of an accident. As she came upon the entrance ramp to the highway, she hesitated. At the last second, she flipped off her blinker and stayed on the country road.

An hour later, she was glad that she had made the decision. The radio station now mentioned an accident that had just occurred on the highway and was telling people to avoid the traffic. She thought it curious that the radio announcer had the time of the accident wrong since the gas station attendant had mentioned it earlier.

She drove along small roads that sent her through farmland and woods. The day was perfect for a drive, with white fluffy clouds dotting the clear blue sky. A strange sense of peace began to settle inside. It was not as though the view outside her windshield was any more or less spectacular than what she had been seeing for the past days of her travels. In truth, she had seen other places that were more breathtaking, the kinds of views that would be found in the background of a movie setting.

No, what she was feeling was different than just an awesome view. She could only describe it as an ease in her chest as though she were coming to the end of a long journey.

According to the GPS, she did not have far to go to get to Richmond. With little plan other than to revisit a place that she had remembered from childhood, she hated the idea of spending another night in a hotel.

GPS guided her down another country lane, woods on either side. *Coming home.* The thought moved through her and she smiled. Traveling slowly as she went around a curve, she spied a 'Cottage For Rent' sign nailed to a mailbox. That was all she could see, considering the house was hidden from the road and trees flanked the gravel driveway.

She flipped on the blinker and turned, the sudden action surprising her. The drive was narrow with thick forest all around. Two cars could have barely passed each other. It curved gently several times before she came to a clearing with a small wooden cabin sitting in the middle of the woods surrounding it. There were no other cars around, and she parked in front. Climbing out, she felt the sun as it beamed onto the little house. She listened to the sound of birds chirping in the trees, and a cool breeze rustled the leaves.

She walked to the front porch that ran the length of the house. Curiosity took over and she peeked through the windows, seeing a small, furnished living room with wooden floors, cream walls, and a stone fireplace. By shifting to the side, she could see a table that led into a U-shaped kitchen. A hall disappeared down the middle, leading to the back where she assumed the bedrooms were. A 'For Rent by Month' sign was tacked to the front door, the real estate agent's phone number listed. *By month?*

She left the porch and walked around to the back, discovering a shaded stone patio with steps that led to a back door. She sat down on one of the steps, resting her elbows on her knees and her chin on her hands. All she could hear was birds singing and the scampering of squirrels near the edge of the trees. Rose bushes, in desperate need of pruning, had been planted at the back of the house.

After years of wanting to escape and weeks of traveling wherever her whims took her, she closed her eyes against the tears that threatened to fall. Whatever she was looking for, it was as though her heart clicked into place at this little cottage. Giving into an impetuous whim, she pulled out her phone and called the agent. Assuring that she was not in a hurry and could wait for him, it was not long before the agent pulled into the drive.

He hopped out of the car, his hand already extended in greeting as he approached. "I'm Dave Porter of Porter Realty. Nice to meet you." As soon as the pleasantries were out of the way, he admitted, "I was so excited to get your call. No one is interested in a small property out this far, even though it's only a fifteen-minute drive into the city. The owner had died, and his children were not ready to sell but wanted to rent instead. Plus, the electricity is already on and there's a well and septic system. Of course, you'd have to get internet service. But the cabin is all clean, nicely furnished, and there's lots of privacy."

He continued his litany of the cabin's virtues as he opened the front door and stepped inside. She tuned him out as she wandered into the living room. Built-in bookcases flanked either side of the fireplace. A wing-back chair sat nearby, angled both toward the fireplace and toward the sofa under the window. As he droned on, she closed her eyes and visualized the bookshelves filled to the brim and a basket of yarn on the floor next to the chair.

Jerking her eyes open, she turned and walked to the dining room, the scarred wooden table surrounded by chairs reminding her of meals lovingly prepared and enjoyed with lively conversation. The cabin was tiny, only two bedrooms and one bathroom, but it was perfect for her. At least for now. At least for a little while. At least while she healed. While she rediscovered who she was.

She questioned him about fees and utilities and confirmed that the owners were willing to rent month-to-month. He had the grace to blush as he admitted that the owners had advertised the cabin for monthly rental, but the fine print stated they required the first and last months' rent as well as a security deposit.

As he handed her forms to fill out, he hovered. "Are you new to the area?"

She glanced up at him as she sat at the table. "I lived not too far from here when I was younger. It was in an older neighborhood, just outside the city. But I have fond memories of that time. I don't know how long I'll be here, so renting month-to-month will be good." *I really want to come back to a place where I was happy.* She did not speak this thought aloud but held it close to her heart. She already felt more at home here in this little cabin than she ever did in California.

His brow furrowed slightly, and he cleared his throat. "Um… what about employment? That is part of the application, as you can see."

"I'm self-employed," she replied. "I'm a writer." She looked up at him and said, "I can provide you with last year's tax statement as proof of income. And I'm prepared to pay in cash."

His brows lifted, and his smile settled once more on his face. "That'll be excellent. The owners are so anxious to rent, I'm sure they'll be fine with you being here."

An hour later, he had taken her money and the signed forms and left her with her copy of the lease and a key. She was surprised that he did not want to do a background check, but she knew money talked. *Like he said... there was probably little interest in a tiny cabin outside the city.*

She had not planned on finding a place to live so quickly but had no remorse over her hasty actions. After having spent years planning everything, she was ready to break free and just live spontaneously. First, her cross-country trip and now, this little house.

Spending the rest of the afternoon unloading her SUV, she heated a can of soup and made a peanut butter and jelly sandwich for supper. Her phone dinged an incoming message. Glancing at it, she immediately shut her phone down. The last thing she needed was unwanted messages.

As the sun moved over the top of the trees and the shadows lengthened in the evening, she pulled books from their boxes and placed them on the shelves. There were not enough books to fill the shelves completely, but just seeing them all together gave her comfort.

She opened the box with the word 'Knitting' written across the top and pulled out her basket, setting it on the floor next to the chair. She filled it with balls of soft, colored yarn and placed her knitting needles within reach.

The room was much smaller than Miss Ethel's, and yet, its familiarity was comforting. Just like with so many times when she was younger, she fixed a cup of tea. Wishing she had milk to go in it, she decided a trip to the grocery store the next day was necessary.

She moved to the back door and walked out onto the

patio, sitting on the step again. The sounds of nature all around were broken only by the muted sound of some kind of machinery in the distance. Not loud enough to be annoying, just present.

Caught up on her writing and editing schedule, she reveled in having several more days before she needed to get back to the current novel she was writing. She planned a trip into the city tomorrow to get cable and internet, grocery shop, and see what else was around. *And maybe, just maybe, take a drive through the old neighborhood for old times' sake.*

Later that night, lying in bed, she read until sleep claimed her. The first peaceful sleep she had had in a very long time.

7

Cas walked from one of the bays into the office of Jayden's garage, J. C. Tire & Auto. Looking over at Ruby, Jayden's wife, he said, "It's all done. She's good to go."

She smiled at him. "That was fast. I know the customer will be glad you were able to take care of it."

He twisted to look over his shoulder at the young mother balancing a toddler on her hip while trying to entertain a bouncy preschooler in the small waiting room. She had brought her minivan in for its inspection, and he'd discovered she needed new brake pads. He had one other car to work on, but since that customer was okay with leaving it, he had immediately gone to work on the minivan.

With a smile and chin lift toward Ruby, he left her to handle the billing with the customer and went back into the garage.

Each of his brothers had found love; several were now parents. Zander had returned from his time in the Army, then bought and ran a bar named Grimm's. He had met his wife, Rosalie, one tragic night at the bar when she was attacked. Now, happily married, they had a little girl. After leaving the Army, Rafe had had a career as a model before leaving the lights of L.A. for the quiet life of being a landscaper. Now, he and his wife, Eleanor, had a son and worked at the veterans burn facility that they had created.

Jaxon was now a paramedic and was married to Morgan, a former Olympic hopeful swimmer who now worked at Eleanor's facility. Zeke had left the military and worked for Zander at Grimm's until he started a restaurant attached to the bar. Zeke and Zander then became partners and had recently expanded to open Grimm's Two. Zeke's fiancé, Cynthia, was their manager.

Cael and Asher were both building contractors, Cael restoring old homes for flipping and Asher owning rental properties. Cael's wife, Regina, worked for a local university, and Asher's wife, Penny, worked as an office manager for a real estate company.

The group got together at Miss Ethel's monthly, sometimes more often. Most of the time Cas made the trip into town to be with them all, but occasionally he missed. Not because he intentionally skipped, but sometimes he would be in his workshop creating furniture and time would simply pass by without him noticing.

He drove the sports car into his bay, already thinking about his evening's activities. Unlike most mechanics, bending over the engine of a sports car gave him no particular thrill. He liked the methodical diagnosis and repair work on engines, and the mechanic's training the Army had given him plus the training he had received from Jayden certainly made him qualified for the job. He enjoyed working for his brother and made good money.

But it was not his passion.

That was reserved for what he could do with wood. Furniture design and building. Self-taught, he spent all of his spare time creating one-of-a-kind pieces. His family had not known of his creations until he finished a project for Miss Ethel, and she showed it off to the others. Jayden had even told him at the time that his efforts at the garage were wasted when he could be building and selling his own line of furniture.

Sure that he would never be able to make a living doing that, he kept his job as a mechanic but occasionally took pieces of furniture to some of the area craft fairs. Ruby designed business cards for him, and he was surprised to see that by the end of the fair, most were gone.

Stunned that each of his pieces sold, he was encouraged by his family to raise his prices. Starting tentatively, he did and was equally surprised that people not only paid for his furniture but were willing to pay well.

He had no desire to make more money than he needed to live off of and save, so he kept his prices reasonable. After a while, some people began special ordering pieces, and for those, he charged more.

An hour later, he finished with the sports car and drove it out of the bay. Cleaning off his hands at the sink, Ruby poked her head out of the door and said,

"Hey, Cas… Jayden would like to see you before you leave."

Wiping his hands on a towel, he jogged up the three steps into the office, seeing Jayden sitting behind his desk. "What's up, bro?"

"You look like shit, Cas," Jayden said, his grin taking the sting out of any insult. Not giving Cas a chance to reply, he asked, "How late are you up at night making furniture?"

Cas glanced over at Ruby, who was attempting an innocent expression while sitting on the stool by the cash register. Plopping into the available chair, he stared at them. "Late."

"I hear you're now taking special orders."

"I've got a couple." From the smile on Ruby's face, he assumed she knew about Rosalie's and Eleanor's friends asking him to design baby beds for their children.

Jayden shook his head. "Cas, I know that's where your heart is. I've always known that. I know you would hate to give up this job, and I sure as hell don't want to make things financially tight for you, but—"

"I'm okay. I mean, I'm not rolling in money, but I've still got savings from when I was in the military."

"Good, good," Jayden said, "because I want you to cut your hours here in the shop. You need more time in your own shop to design and build furniture, and the only way you're going to have that time is to cut back here."

Tamping down the excitement of having days that he could spend in his workshop, he asked, "What kind of cutback are you talking about?"

Shrugging his shoulders with his hands lifted to his sides, Jayden looked to him. "You tell me. Cas, I want this to work for you. My business is good. I can bring on a part-time or a full-time mechanic."

Rubbing his chin, he quickly calculated the hours it would take each week to work on the projects that were coming in. Excitement bubbled deep inside, starting slow and building, He was no longer able to keep his grin from widening. Holding Jayden's gaze, he said, "It would be good if I could have two full days off a week to just work in my workshop."

Jayden lifted an eyebrow in doubt. "Just two?"

"Let's start with that and see how it goes," Cas suggested. The two men took to their feet at the same time, hands reaching out to clasp. "Thanks, Jayden. This means a lot to me."

Ruby slipped off the stool and walked around to Jayden, her arm sliding around her husband's waist as she smiled up at Cas. "See you there?"

He knew she was referring to the dinner at Miss Ethel's, and he nodded. "Yeah, that's where I'm heading right now."

Saying goodbye, he walked out to his truck and spent the drive to Miss Ethel's busily planning his next project. Parking at her house, he glanced across the street as he always did. It was a habit… just like looking at the trees in the corner where he used to spend time whittling or writing or the other millions of memories that he had at her house.

Seeing that he was the first one to arrive, he jogged up the front porch steps and into the house. Hearing a noise from the kitchen, he made his way past the living room and dining room, down the hall, and into the large room that Miss Ethel felt was the hub of her house.

She looked up from the pot she was stirring and her warm smile greeted him. Her hair was now white, pulled back in a bun. Her eyes, more grey than blue, still twinkled from behind her wire-rimmed glasses. Her frame, even more thin, was encased in a buttery yellow dress, belted at the waist. As always, she immediately turned from whatever she was doing and opened her arms.

Never turning down her silent invitation, he walked into her embrace. One thing he noticed was that her arms never seemed to weaken. Her hug was just as firm. He inhaled deeply the light scent of rose water, so familiar and so comforting at the same time.

"Oh, my Cas," she said. Leaning back, she looked up at him, then tilted her head slightly to the side. "You look like a man with news to tell."

He had no idea how she did that… how she knew just by looking at one of them that there was something going on in their lives. It was a mystery not to be discovered, so he did not question it. Grinning, he nodded. "Jayden and I talked today. I'm cutting back my hours at the garage so that I'll have more time at my own workshop."

Her delight was obvious, and she said, "Oh, I am glad. Cas, my boy, you're so talented and so deserving. I've always wanted my boys to follow their passion, and building furniture is definitely your calling."

The sound of the front door opening was heard, and soon the house was filled with all of his brothers and their wives and children. He scooped up Zander's little girl, Charity, blowing raspberries on her belly, much to her delight. Then he moved over to Eleanor, kissed her cheek and Rory's head, and said, "I'm glad you liked his bed. The one for your friend will be ready soon. In fact, since I'm going to have a few extra days a week to work on it, I should have it by this weekend."

Ruby was spreading the news of Cas having full days to work on his furniture, and he accepted the congratulations from the gathering. Shooting Jayden a grin which he hoped showed his gratitude, he sat down at the table after helping Miss Ethel bring out the food.

As usual, the meal was filled with lots of conversation, sharing about lives, reminisces of the past.

"Do you remember that girl that lived across the street for a while? Bianca?" Rafe asked. "I thought about her the other day when I was reading to Rory. I remembered what she said about the prince in Snow White. How he just stumbled upon her and hadn't done anything to deserve her, and it was the huntsman that had truly saved her."

"And how the dwarfs were her friends," Jaxon laughed.

"Wonder whatever happened to her," Zeke said, passing a bowl to Cynthia.

Miss Ethel's brow furrowed. "I don't know. She and her father moved away about the time the last of you graduated. I had hoped to hear from her after they left but never did."

"You were close to her, Cas," Jayden said, looking over at him. "Did she ever get in contact with you?"

Shaking his head, he replied, "I left for the Army right when she moved. We never had contact after that." Regret shot through him like a bolt, and he lifted his hand and rubbed his chest.

"In this day and age of social media, you could probably find out about her," Regina commented.

He had thought about it before, but something always held him back. Maybe it was the lack of desire to see her life as she moved away from him. Continuing to shake his head, he lied, "Nah. She was just a girl I knew as a kid. Nothing more."

Rafe said, "It was weird to suddenly have that memory jump back into my head."

Zander piped up, "I think it's because you're a father. Seriously, there's all kinds of things that now come to mind." He nodded toward Miss Ethel. "I find myself wanting to remember everything about growing up with you so that I can try to do the right things with Charity."

The conversation around the table moved to their childhood memories, most tales spent one-upping each other. But for Cas, he thought of Bianca. Her black hair, pale complexion, blue eyes, and the way she made him feel. She would listen… really listen to whatever was on his mind. She had a way of making him feel as though he could do anything.

He zoned out what the others were saying, startling when there was more laughter around the table and realized he had missed the last story. His eyes jumped to

Miss Ethel's and found them on him, her gaze thoughtful.

He stayed back after the others left, checking to make sure she had everything she needed. She lifted her hand and patted his cheek, saying, "All my good boys have grown into such good men."

They stepped out on the front porch together, and as though a magnet drew their eyes, both looked across the street.

"You remember young Bianca better than you let on during dinner." Her voice was soft, without judgment. But her intuition was, as always, correct.

His hand drifted upward to rub his chest again. He could never lie to Miss Ethel and was not about to begin now. "I do remember her very well. We had… well, I guess you'd call it a special friendship." A heavy sigh slipped from his lips. " We were very young, though. Like I said, she's a pleasant memory from my childhood."

She smiled indulgently. "She was such a delight to have around. So very intuitive for such a young person."

"Yeah, she was. Funny, smart."

"I used to call her an old soul," Miss Ethel remembered.

"Sometimes I wondered what all was going on in her head. She was always creating characters and stories."

"In many ways, you two were so much alike. Both inventive… creative… artistic."

He had not thought of their similarities, and the idea caused his lips to curve. Giving his head a little shake, he tightened his arm and squeezed her shoulders. "I'm going to head on home now, Miss Ethel. I've got furniture to build and all day tomorrow to be able to work on it."

"Of all my boys, I should've known that you would end up with a cabin in the woods, surrounded by your workshop and the nature you always loved ."

He grinned and nodded. "A house in the city was never going to be for me. I love my cabin. Plenty of privacy. Plenty of quiet for me to be able to design my furniture. And if I'm in the mood to stay up all night and build, I don't disturb anyone."

Bending, he kissed her cheek and jogged down the steps toward his truck.

Miss Ethel stood on the porch and waved goodbye, her smile staying on her face long after his truck disappeared down the road. A breeze blew past, the wind whispering in her ear. With a twinkle in her eyes, she moved back inside her house.

8

Driving home, Cas' mind was on the baby bed he was building. He had made one for Rafe's son, Rory, using designs he had found online for a child's bed that could go from a crib to a junior bed, and made it his own by adding carvings of an enchanted forest in the headboard. A friend of Eleanor's had seen it and wanted one like it.

As he neared his drive, he noticed the 'For Rent' sign was missing from the property next to his. He had bought his cabin property two years ago, and the elderly man who lived next to him had died soon after. He had been aware that work was being done on the cabin and the man's children were hoping to sell it. When that did not happen, they decided to rent it, but it had sat empty for a while.

Turning into his own drive, he curved around the gravel lane before coming to his cabin in the clearing. The two-story dwelling had needed minor repairs when he first discovered it, but with Asher and Cael's expertise and the hard work of the rest of his brothers, it had been restored beautifully, even adding a connecting garage. By doing a lot of the work themselves, he had been able to build a large workshop behind the house without a lot of extra costs.

At first thinking small, he was thankful that his brothers had convinced him to go ahead and make it a large workshop. It held space for all of his woodworking tools and equipment as well as giving him a dry space for storing the wood that he purchased for his builds. It also included a full-size drafting table where he could create his designs.

Parking in the garage, he walked into the utility room and was greeted by a solid-white cat with blue eyes. He bent to rub her head, murmuring his greeting. "Hey, Princess." The cat looked up at him as he patted her, arching her back and flicking the end of her tail. He always greeted her the same way, and even though she was deaf, he still called her 'Princess' out of habit.

She kept her eyes on him as he moved into the kitchen, swirling about his legs as he fixed her bowl with her food. He tried to stick to a schedule, knowing that made it easier for her to know what was going on. Once she was fed, he moved to his refrigerator and grabbed a beer before heading out to his workshop.

Jayden often kept music on in the garage, although at times it could barely be heard over the noise of engines and machinery. With all four bays being filled on most days, the noise and activity could be distracting.

But out here, Cas reveled in the quiet around him,

the only noise coming from whatever machine he was using at the time or perhaps soft music. As he sanded over the wood, he planned his next day now that he did not have to go into the garage. Looking at the head-board, he knew that if he could finish it tonight, he would have tomorrow to stain it.

His movements were skillful and practiced, and he allowed his mind to wander. And it drifted back to his teen years with Bianca. Talking with her as they sat in the front yard, his hands busy with whittling and she plucking little yellow flowers and tying their stems together. *Jesus, I haven't thought of that in years.*

Hours later, the bed was finished except for staining. He spent time cleaning the shop, not wanting to become buried in sawdust or wood chips. *"Son, make sure you sweep up all the sawdust, or it'll soon cover everything in here."* His father had given him the job of sweeping the floor of his workshop, keeping it tidy. He could still hear his father's words and was grateful his wisdom was passed down through the years.

Walking back over to the headboard, he ran his palm over the smooth wood, his fingers dipping into the divots of the carvings of the forest with a little boy and girl peeking from behind the trees.

He felt a sense of satisfaction that working on a car never gave him. Certainly, diagnosing and fixing an automotive problem had its own reward, but here in his workshop was where he could imagine, create, and bring something to life that had before just been wood.

Not for the first time he wondered if his father would be proud. Smiling as his hands skimmed over the headboard, he knew the answer to that question would be… abso-fucking-lutely. His father had loved his craft, often telling Cas that throughout history man had worked with wood, whether for practical functions, hunting, warfare, or art. To learn the skills used to turn trees into works of art was something to be proud of, and to do it by hand in modern times was a craft slowly dying.

Staring at the carving of Hansel and Gretel, he realized that subconsciously they represented he and Bianca. Granted, they were not little children when they met, but the copse of trees in the corner of Miss Ethel's yard had become their place. Miss Ethel was right this evening when she said that he remembered Bianca more than he let on.

When she left Virginia, it was as though she fell off the ends of the earth. A week later, he left for boot camp, and his world became his Army buddies, keeping up with his brothers wherever they were stationed, and checking on Miss Ethel. He had cared for Bianca and thought maybe they had a future, but those were the dreams of a very young man, still in his teens. *There had been the one letter sent…* He squeezed his eyes shut tightly for a few seconds, remembering how the embarrassing rebuttal that came back had cut right through him.

Regina was right… he could have searched for her in later years with social media, but by the time he finished his years in the Army, he chose not to. After all he had gone through, he could not see the point of reaching back through the years to grasp onto something that had been settled securely in the past.

There had been other women, ones who came and went in his life, some for a few months, some for a night. But, unlike his brothers, he had never met anyone that he considered to be a soulmate. *Maybe there's only one of those in a lifetime... and I knew her as a teen.*

With a final smooth of his hand over the wood, he sighed and closed the workshop, going back inside his house.

"I'm back, Mom."

Bianca had come into town to shop but first gave in to the overwhelming desire to visit her mother's gravesite. It was just as she remembered. ***Beloved wife and mother*** graced the tombstone. Kneeling, her fingers traced over the familiar carved marble.

She had already made arrangements for her father's ashes to be interred next to her mother, and the simple ceremony would be next week. That would finally lay to rest her parents together and would also end the reign of Lucille's terror.

"I know he's already with you, Mom." She lifted her face to the sun and smiled as the warmth filled her.

Bianca did not visit the old neighborhood since finding the cemetery and shopping took most of the day. Once she was back inside her cabin, her time was filled with putting away her purchases and groceries and giving the cabin a good scrubbing.

She was tired when she finished, but that was something that often affected her. She lifted her hand, her fingers lightly tracing the scar that ran down the middle of her chest.

She spent the late afternoon working on her manuscript, glad to have a career where she could work from home. Editing for others had led to her finally deciding to write her own books and self-publish. *All the stories and characters in my head finally have a home inside a book.*

Her romance stories were a combination of fairy tales with twists, often with suspense mixed into the plots. An old-fashioned cuckoo clock on the wall chimed and she sat up straight, stretching her arms over her head. Determining she was at a good place to stop, she saved her manuscript and shut her computer before finally retiring to the living room. The chair was comfortable, and she tucked her legs up under her.

She snagged her knitting from the basket on the floor, smiling as the needles clicked a rapid rhythm. Knitting was a task learned many years ago. One she could perform as she allowed her mind to roll through the stories and characters that filled her head. Sometimes she was surprised to realize that she had been knitting continuously without giving much consideration to the pattern she was creating.

Life had not taken her where she had thought it would go, but she was no longer willing to settle for what others wanted. She had done that for her father. She had done that for her stepmother. And she had certainly done that when she became ill, putting all of her dreams aside.

Now, it was time for her. Placing her knitting back

into the basket, she moved into the kitchen and fixed a cup of herbal tea. Taking it to the back patio, she sat on the steps as she had done the previous evening. Her phone dinged another incoming message, but she quickly turned the sound down on her phone. There was no one who would be contacting her that she cared to talk to. Or hear from.

Leaning back, she sipped her tea and let the sounds of the evening in the forest move through her. She could hear the humming of equipment in the background and wondered what the neighbor was working on.

She considered walking through the woods to see if she could meet them, but it was already getting dark, and she did not want to run into a neighbor who did not want to be disturbed.

Her tea finished, she went back inside and soon crawled into bed. Thinking about the old neighborhood, she remembered the street that she and her father lived on. *Tomorrow... I shall go tomorrow. Just for old times' sake.* While she could not remember the last name of the wonderful woman who had lived across the street, she had no trouble remembering her first name. Ethel. The amazing Miss Ethel. Just thinking of her made Bianca smile.

Snuggling under the covers, she allowed her thoughts to drift once again to Cas. It had been many years since she was a young teenager falling for the handsome boy across the street. She wondered where he was and if she ever crossed his mind when he thought back to his youth.

Bianca had never spent much time on social media and never attempted to stalk him. When her youthful dreams were taken away, she had no desire to see him moving on with his life. Sighing, she rolled over and re-fluffed her pillow, trying to find a comfortable position. Finally exhausted, she fell asleep.

The next morning dawned bright and clear, and she felt invigorated. After an early morning breakfast of cereal and a cup of herbal tea, she was ready to go. It was only a twenty-minute drive to the old neighborhood. Along the way, she passed by the high school where she had started before she and her dad had moved to California.

I must have been the envy of every girl there when I walked in each day with the eight most handsome guys at school. She stopped and stared at the building, memories washing over her. Cas walking her to class. Meeting with all of them after school. Watching them play ball. Cheering for Cas when he ran cross-country. Giving her head a little shake, she pulled back onto the road.

She turned down several streets, thinking that she might need to use GPS, but found that the way was familiar. Once on her old road, she drove slowly. The houses on either side of the road did nothing to bring forth any memories, but as she approached the end of the cul-de-sac, her breath caught in her throat as she spied her old house. Freshly painted, with flower boxes in the windows, she smiled at the sight of children's bicycles in the front yard.

Her memories were filled with her dad as he tried to make a good home for her. He was often gone for work, but when they were together, they had fun. She knew he had missed her mom, but after her mom's death, Bianca thought she and her dad had forged their own little family of two. *I thought we would stay here, Dad. I wanted us to stay here.* But that was before Lucille. *He had been so determined to give me a stepmother.* Inwardly growling, she pushed thoughts of Lucille from her mind.

Turning her head to look at the very end of the cul-de-sac, she viewed the large, two-story home that she remembered so well. The picket fence was in good repair, freshly painted. It appeared the house and porch were equally well-tended. The trees in the corner of the yard still stood, and she remembered the hours sitting there with Cas as they talked.

Looking back, she was amazed that a thirteen-year-old boy would have spent time talking to an eleven-year-old girl. *Oh, my... I was such a little dork. Dancing and singing in the yard.* She put her vehicle in park as memories flooded over her. Even his brothers, older and bigger, had never treated her as though she were a pest.

And Miss Ethel's comforting presence had always made Bianca feel welcome. She thought about the four years that she and her dad lived across from this house, and how in many ways Cas' family was like her own. She had had big dreams... she had written Cas' name in her notebooks hundreds of times and thought that she would be waiting right there for him when he got back from the military. Rolling her eyes, she scoffed at the folly of youth. Even her one letter sent to Cas, care of Miss Ethel, had brought no reply.

She sighed as she started her vehicle and glanced into her rearview mirror, making sure there were no other cars coming. From that angle, her father's house was what she saw in the mirror, and she closed her eyes for a few seconds. It seemed like she was always looking behind her. She opened her eyes as she gave her head a little shake. *No more... from now on I want to look forward.*

Sucking in a cleansing breath, she let it out slowly and pressed on the accelerator. Out of the front windshield, she observed a woman stepping out onto the porch of the house in front of her. Blinking to assure that she was not dreaming, she recognized Miss Ethel. Slamming on the brakes, she stopped and watched as Miss Ethel, older but so familiar, began watering the hanging baskets.

Drawn by an invisible magnet that she knew was connected to her past, she put her SUV in park, shut down the engine, and stepped out. She walked up the front sidewalk toward the porch on unsteady legs. Just as Miss Ethel turned toward her, she called out, "Miss Ethel? I don't know if you remember me but—"

Miss Ethel set the watering can onto the porch and peered carefully at her. Then, gasping, she exclaimed, "Bianca! Bianca Winters!"

Miss Ethel opened her arms wide, and Bianca found herself running into the older woman's embrace. Holding on tightly, it was as though time stood still, and she relished the warm comfort that Miss Ethel had always provided.

Finally, Miss Ethel's arms loosened, and Bianca stepped back. Wiping the tears that had gathered in her eyes, she smiled. "I had no idea you'd still be living here!"

"Oh, my dear, in a life where things are changing daily, some things never do. I'm not sure I can ever see myself living anywhere else." Miss Ethel held her at arm's length and asked, "But what are you doing here?"

Shrugging, she replied, "I just came to see the old neighborhood."

"Oh, I have so many questions!" Miss Ethel said, her smile as warm as Bianca remembered. "Do you have time for a cup of tea?"

"I've got plenty of time for a cup of tea," she replied. Giving Miss Ethel's hands a squeeze, she said, "I can't think of anything I'd like better right now."

Following Miss Ethel into her home, Bianca had the strange sensation that the past, the present, and the future were sliding into place together.

9

Stepping over the threshold, Bianca sucked in her lips as she looked at the living room she so vividly remembered, and, in fact, tried to replicate with her cabin. Miss Ethel's sofa had been updated, still appearing comfortable but in a deep green and burgundy pattern. Even the wingback chair next to the knitting basket was new. The seat cushion was indented, but the burgundy color worked so well with the new sofa.

The end tables and coffee table were the same, and as she stood in the middle of the room, she deeply inhaled the soft scent of rose water.

Miss Ethel turned to her and said, "I'm afraid the house has not changed much, other than it's just me here now, of course. Come on back to the kitchen with me, and I'll fix the tea."

She eagerly followed Miss Ethel down the hall, past the large dining room whose table now appeared even longer. Once inside the kitchen, she recognized that it had also been updated with new appliances and countertops. The warm oak cabinets were still the same, and she found herself glad that some of the old still remained with the new.

For a few minutes, she quietly looked around as Miss Ethel made a pot of tea. Once it was placed on a tea tray with two cups and a plate of cookies, she stepped forward and picked it up. She carried it for Miss Ethel back into the living room, placing it on the coffee table

After they poured the tea, she said, "I have to ask you, Miss Ethel. How on earth did you recognize me?"

Miss Ethel's eyes danced as they moved over Bianca. "Your hair is longer now, but it was always so black and sleek. And your eyes are such a deep blue. I think, my dear, that I would've recognized you anywhere."

She sipped the warm tea and settled into the deep sofa cushions. Her gaze moved to the bookcase flanking the fireplace, still filled with the volumes that had been lovingly read and passages memorized. There were new pictures, some with women, but she was too far away to see them clearly. She wanted to ask about the boys, but uncertainty held her back.

"So, tell me," Miss Ethel began, "How's your father?"

Her gaze dropped from the bookshelf to Miss Ethel, and she sighed. "My father died last year."

Miss Ethel's brow furrowed, and her smile fell away. "Oh, Bianca, I am so sorry."

Swallowing deeply, she nodded her acceptance of Miss Ethel's condolences. "He'd been sick for a long time. Cancer. In the end, his death was a blessing. I knew then he was at peace." She took another sip, hesitating before adding, "My stepmother, Lucille, had made things very... um... well... um... difficult."

"Ah, yes. I remember Lucille. I used to wonder if she ever got what she was looking for," Miss Ethel stated, showing neither surprise nor censure.

Bianca was curious about that comment, but as she sat for a moment, she realized that there were things Miss Ethel would have discerned about Lucille that she had never seen as a teenager. Nodding, she replied, "Yes, initially, I think she did. Lucille loved attention, and when Dad married her, he seemed quite... smitten with her." Giving her head a little shake, she smirked, "Smitten is such an old-fashioned word, and yet, it seemed to fit my father perfectly."

Peering at her closely, Miss Ethel stated, "And you were never quite so smitten."

A small snort erupted, and Bianca blushed. "I was definitely *not* smitten. Lucille was a rather... um... singular person. Someone who preferred to not share her husband's attention or affection. She wanted Dad to give her more. Take her places. Spend money on her. I sometimes think she wanted him to show her off. She was very vain. Very demanding. Sometimes even very demeaning."

"I am sorry, Bianca." Miss Ethel's voice was soft, and she cocked her head slightly to the side. "And yet you stayed in California. Was that because of your father?"

She glanced out the window toward her former house across the street and remembered how nice it was before Lucille. *So much was nicer before Lucille. If not for her, we would have never moved and then maybe...*

Turning her attention back to Miss Ethel, she immediately felt the warmth and concern radiating from the older woman, so unlike her stepmother. Sucking in a deep breath, she let it out slowly. "I felt as though my father was blind to Lucille's machinations, and I didn't trust her. In the end, I'm glad I stayed. My father and I grew closer as he began to see her true colors." Pinching her lips together, she fought to keep her anger inside. Letting the breath out slowly, she added, "But now, I'm free to live my life."

"And you came back to visit the old neighborhood," Miss Ethel declared, once more smiling as she clapped her hands. "How lovely!"

Still wanting to ask about the boys, she remained quiet. *Is wondering about Cas' life worse than possibly knowing I had no place in it?*

As though picking up on her hesitation, Miss Ethel said, "You must be curious about everybody."

"Yes, actually, I am. I drove by my house and had no thoughts about me and Dad living there that didn't involve your welcoming home. I think you and this house are what I really wanted to see." She paused for a few seconds and closed her eyes, listening carefully. In her mind, she could hear the sounds of boys' laughter ringing through the halls. But in truth, the walls were only filled with memories and not activity. She opened her eyes and knew her smile was sad. "It's so quiet now."

Chuckling, Miss Ethel agreed. "I'm sure everyone thinks that after having all my boys, I must relish the quiet. Actually, I find that silence is sometimes annoying. I tell myself that the quiet is a good thing because it reminds me that all my boys are happy, healthy, grown, and living their own lives. I suppose that's the best a parent can hope for in their old age when the quiet seems to close in on them and memories take over."

Nodding slowly, she said, "I understand what you mean. It seems like I spend a lot of my time looking back at the past. It's only been recently that I started looking forward."

"And yet you came back to Virginia..."

"I suppose I needed to come back to where I was last happy. I traveled through lots of states on my way here, knowing I could stop anywhere to settle for a while. But until I reached back and touched my past, I couldn't move forward."

Miss Ethel's eyes appeared to water, and she blinked several times. "Oh, my dear, you have such a gift with words. That's beautiful."

Her heart sang at the praise. "I have a confession. I'm a writer now."

"Now I have someone new I can quote!" Miss Ethel clapped her hands in delight.

"I always loved your quotes! I think you are what inspired me."

"And I used to tell the boys that not only did you have a vivid imagination, but you were so insightful. Older than your years."

They smiled at each other, taking more sips of tea. Miss Ethel inclined her head toward the picture frames on the bookshelves. "All of my boys came back from the military and landed nearby."

Interest, which she had held to a simmer, flared to

life, and she sucked in a rapid breath. "Oh, please tell me about them. About them all."

As though settling in to talk about her favorite subject — which Bianca had no doubt was true — Miss Ethel began. "Zander was the first to leave and the first to return. Being the oldest of my boys, I think he always felt a sense of responsibility for the others. He never talked much about his time in the Army, but I have no doubt he carried that same sense of responsibility to the men and women he worked with. When he came back, he seemed a bit lost until he decided to buy an old run-down bar, refurbished it, and opened Grimm's."

Eyes bugging out of her head, Bianca cackled with laughter. "He named his bar after the Grimm brothers?"

Nodding, Miss Ethel's lips curved as well. "I'm sure that many of the patrons of his establishment have no idea the significance behind the name." Her voice softened, and she said, "He's now married to a lovely teacher named Rosalie, and they have a little girl, Charity."

It was not hard for Bianca to imagine the serious Zander owning his own business but being married with a little girl was something she hoped she would be able to see.

Continuing, Miss Ethel said, "Zeke is a partner with Zander, and he runs the restaurant. Cael came back and owns his own business restoring old houses. He and Asher, who is also in construction, do a lot of work together. Asher helped get one of our local homeless shelters started, a place where Zeke donates a lot of time as well. Rafe works with his wife at a burn center she developed. Jaxon is a paramedic, and Jayden owns his own garage."

Bianca thought of how close the boys were when she knew them as teenagers, and it appeared they had that same bond as adults. Looking up at Miss Ethel who was staring at her, she said, "I'm really glad the boys are still close. I think that's wonderful." It had not skipped her notice that no mention of Cas had been made. Her heart squeezed, and she licked her dry lips.

Before she had a chance to ask, Miss Ethel continued, "Yes, the boys are very close. In fact, Cas works for Jayden at the garage."

The air left her lungs in a rush at hearing his name leave Miss Ethel's lips. She once again felt Miss Ethel's assessing gaze and hurried to ask, "And, they're all... um... well?"

Miss Ethel took another sip of tea, drawing out her answer, making Bianca squirm. Setting her teacup down, Miss Ethel nodded. "Yes, they're all well. In fact, they're all married with the exception of Cas."

Hearing that Cas was not married caused her heart to leap. Tamping down that feeling, she knew that did not mean he was not involved with someone. Before she had a chance to learn more, Miss Ethel glanced at the clock.

"Oh, I'm so sorry. I have someone coming to pick me up to take me to a church meeting. But you must come back soon. The boys would love to see you again!"

Smiling, she could not contain the excitement of seeing them as well.

"The boys made sure that I have a cell phone," Miss

Ethel said as she pulled it from her pocket. "They're afraid if I don't have it with me, I might fall in the garden and lay there amongst my roses until someone discovered me!"

Thinking that was a smart idea, she said, "I can put my phone number in it along with my name, and then you'll have it."

She quickly programmed her number into Miss Ethel's phone and then accepted a call back so that she could have Miss Ethel's information in return. Standing, she took the tea tray into the kitchen and placed it on the counter. "Would you like me to wash these?"

Miss Ethel waved her hand dismissively, and said, "Oh, goodness gracious no. That will give me something to occupy myself with when I come back from my meeting." Walking her to the door, Miss Ethel held onto Bianca's arm. "I didn't even ask where you're staying."

"I'm afraid I've been rather impetuous," she declared. "I was driving toward Richmond, and my GPS had me on a little country road because there was an accident on the highway. I passed through some woods and there was a 'For Rent' sign. On a complete whim, I took a look at the house, called the realtor, and discovered it was a darling little cabin that was already furnished and is being rented by the month. It's about fifteen miles away on the west side of town. I rented that very day. I spent the last two days making sure it was fixed up and had groceries, so I'm well settled, at least for a month until I decide what I want to do."

"Are you in a neighborhood?"

Shaking her head, she said, "No, it's truly just a

country road. Hunter Lane. In fact, I only have one neighbor that I know of. It's very quiet and isolated."

Miss Ethel stilled, her hands halting as they reached for her purse, and she stared at Bianca. Her lips curved into a slow smile, and she said, "You have no idea how glad I am that you stopped by today. It's been lovely to talk to you, and I can't wait until you get a chance to be with all my boys again." She bent to pick up her purse, and the two women walked out onto the front porch, Miss Ethel locking the door behind her.

They walked down the front walk toward the car that had arrived to pick up Miss Ethel. She turned and looked at Bianca again, gave her a warm hug, and said, "Perhaps you should meet your neighbor. After all, 'Never look too far to find a family. Your neighbor is your closest family.'" Miss Ethel appeared bemused and added, "I was actually reading something Mr. Rogers had written about neighbors, and came across a brilliant young woman, Lailah Gifty Akita, who had said something very similar." Shrugging her thin shoulders, she laughed. "I'm never sure anymore what quotes will pop out of my mouth!"

Kissing Bianca's cheek, she climbed into her friend's car, leaving Bianca on the sidewalk, waiting until she was out of sight. She leaned her head back and let the warmth of the sun fall on her face. Looking back, it felt as though life has been such a battle for so many years, and now, a new chance at happiness was awaiting.

Climbing into her small SUV, she drove out of the city toward Hunter Lane. She glanced at her neighbor's driveway, and like hers, it disappeared into the woods so she could not see the house. She continued on to her drive, excited to see the small cabin come into view.

The tea and cookies with Miss Ethel had been delightful but did little to assuage her hunger. Fixing a sandwich, she went out to her patio, sitting on the step with her plate balanced on her knees.

Halfway through her meal, a yowling close by startled her. Jerking her head to the side, she saw a sleek, solid white cat standing under a bush staring at her. Or, perhaps, staring at her sandwich.

"Where did you come from?" She held her hand out, and the cat walked forward and sniffed her fingers. "Oh, my, you are beautiful." She stroked the silky fur, scratched under her chin, and rubbed her ears. She remembered reading that white cats were often deaf, and when she snapped her fingers behind its head, the cat made no indication that it heard. "You couldn't have come far," she said, noting the cat's clean fur, clear eyes, and healthy weight.

Not wanting the cat to be in danger outside, she coaxed it into her house with nibbles from her sandwich. "Come on in, and I'll check with my neighbor to see if that's who you belong to."

The cat sat on her haunches in the middle of the kitchen, looked at her, then began washing its face.

After closing her back door securely, Bianca walked to the edge of her clearing and stared through the forest of trees toward her neighbor's land. Her lot was large, covering several acres according to the real estate agent, but since her neighbor's driveway was close to hers, she assumed their house would not be too great a distance.

As she walked through the woods, she was soon able to see a large, wooden building and made her way toward it. Exiting the woods from the back, she walked around to the side and saw that it was almost like a garage, with her neighbor's house sitting closer to the drive on the other side of their clearing.

Curious as to the sounds she had been hearing at night, she headed straight to one of the windows, placed her forehead against the glass with her hands cupped around her eyes, and peered inside. It was a workshop, and from what she could see it contained unfinished and finished pieces of furniture. Walking around the building, she looked toward the house but did not see anyone around.

Glancing back at the workshop, she observed that the door was partially opened. She called out but received no answer. Pushing the door open a little further, her eyes landed on the headboard of a small bed, one that would fit a child. Intricate carvings captured her attention and she moved forward, pulled inward by the desire to inspect it closer, even though she knew she was snooping. A little boy and girl appeared to be peeking from behind carved trees toward a gingerbread house in the distance. *Hansel and Gretel!*

Captivated, she gently reached out. Her fingers touched the smooth wood, and she was bewitched by the workmanship in front of her. Unheeding of the fact that she was trespassing, she continued to walk around the workshop, seeing other pieces of furniture. There were chairs and tables and another child's bed, this time with the carvings of a sleeping princess, a prince kneeling nearby. *Sleeping Beauty!*

The cat and her mission were forgotten as she stood and admired the work, wondering about the talent of the woodsman.

10

Cas had spent the morning in his workshop, applying a second coat of stain to the Hansel and Gretel bed. Once satisfied, he headed inside his house for lunch, then spent time at his computer looking through some of the marketing plans Cael had sent to him. Regina had created a website to show the restoration work Cael did on old homes and recently suggested that Cas have a website for his handmade furniture.

Tired of looking at various sites, he leaned back in his chair and stretched his arms above his head. It dawned on him that he had not seen Princess since he came back into the house. She often disappeared, finding a sunny corner to sleep in, but never missed a meal.

He began searching room by room but was unable to locate her. His concern ratcheted up with every moment she remained unfound. He had raised his bedroom window overnight to allow a breeze to come through. Princess often liked to sit on the windowsill, sniffing the fresh air. Moving to his window, he was stunned to see that the screen was loose from its frame, creating an opening that had bits of white fur caught in it.

Horrified that she might have gotten outside to chase something she spied, he raced through his house and out the back door. He had no idea how to locate her since her deafness kept him from calling out.

Heart pounding, he raced around the perimeter of his house, not seeing her. Looking toward the edge of the clearing where his workshop stood, he noticed the door was pushed open further than he had left it. *Oh, thank God! She's in there!*

Feet pounding over the grass, he ran to his workshop, threw the door open wider and darted inside, kicking the door behind him to make sure she did not escape. Instead of seeing Princess, there was a woman standing with her back against the window, her fingers resting on one of the children's beds he had made.

Stunned, his body jerked as his feet came to a sudden halt. "Who the hell are you?" he bit out, his gaze moving from her to the floor to see if his cat was skulking about.

He heard the woman squeak, but with the dim light in his shop, her face was in shadow and he could not discern her features clearly. Her eyes opened wide and her hand snatched back from the wood as though burned.

Taking a step forward, he repeated, "Who the hell are you?"

"I'm so sorry." The woman's voice was rushed,

carrying an element of fear. "I know I'm trespassing, but I came over to find out about a cat and I saw the door open—"

His gaze had bounced between her and scanning the floor to see if he could see Princess, but now jerked back to the woman's face. "Cat? What about my cat?"

"A white cat came to my house and I was trying to find the owner—"

"What house? Where do you live?" he barked.

Huffing, the woman sighed. "Look, I know I'm trespassing, and I've apologized. But please, let me explain, and if the cat is yours, then I can get it for you."

Fists on his hips, he continued to glare but stayed quiet, waiting for her to speak.

"I just moved in next door… the rental. A solid white cat came up to my back patio. I could tell she was somebody's pet because she was well-fed and beautiful. This was the only other house I knew that was around here. I put her inside my house so that she would be safe and walked over here." She looked around, and her hands lifted to her sides as she continued, "I confess that when I saw the door open and came in, I was absolutely entranced by the work you do."

"The cat is mine," he stated. Turning to the side, he waved his arm toward the door as though inviting her to leave in front of him. "I'd like to go get her now if you don't mind." He knew he was being rude but worry over Princess caused his words to continue to carry a bite.

The woman did not move but cocked her head to the side. "How do I know that the cat is yours?"

He tried to keep from growling, but his fear for his

cat was now morphing into anger. "White cat. Female. Blue eyes. Deaf."

The woman's shoulders relaxed, and she nodded. "That's right. I can go get her and bring her—"

"I'll come."

"Oh... okay." The woman walked past him, keeping her gaze straight ahead as they left the shadowed interior of the workshop. She continued to walk into the woods, and he followed right behind. She was shorter than him, only coming to his shoulder, and her body was slender. Not too thin like she starved herself every meal nor overly athletic as though she worked out at the gym every day. She had curves, and his eyes dropped to the way her shorts cupped her ass.

"There isn't a path between our houses, but I found that it wasn't far," she called out, not even looking over her shoulder at him.

He was glad she was staring straight ahead so that he was not caught ogling her ass. Forcing his gaze upward, he noticed her shiny, black hair swinging just below her shoulders. They quickly came out of the woods and into a clearing similar to his own. Her cabin was much smaller than his and without a garage. He followed her to her back patio and halted as she started into her house.

As much as he wanted to get to his cat, he was not about to enter a woman's house uninvited. The screen door slammed shut behind her and she called out, "It's okay, you can come in."

With his hand on the screen door, he asked, "Are you

sure? You can just bring Princess to me, and I'll take her off your hands and get her back home."

The woman had bent behind the kitchen counter and now walked back toward the door, cradling the large white cat in her arms. He was staring at Princess, breathing a sigh of relief, and with a wide smile now on his face, he opened the door. Stepping inside her house, he extended his arms.

"Oh, my God!" the woman said as she stumbled backward.

His gaze shot up to her face as the screen door slammed closed behind him, and Princess jumped to the floor at the movement. The woman's blue eyes were wide, her black hair framing her pale face. It took several seconds for his mind to catch up to what his eyes were seeing, then he repeated her words, "Oh, my God." Princess, now forgotten at their feet, walked away, swishing her tail.

"Cas?"

"Bianca?"

He moved forward on instinct as she threw her arms around him. Stunned that someone he thought he would never see now had their arms around him and was tucked underneath his chin, his mind raced with questions. Hers must have also because she leaned back, peered up at him, and said, "I can't believe it's you!"

She lowered her arms and stepped back, and he instantly missed her touch. Her gaze moved over him in the same way that his had earlier when he checked her out.

They both started to speak at the same time, then

halted and laughed. "I don't even know where to start," he said, shaking his head slowly. "I never thought I'd see you again."

"I wanted to see you," she admitted, and he remembered how openly honest she had been when she was younger. It seemed like that trait was still very much a part of her. "I even went by your old house today and saw Miss Ethel."

"You're kidding!"

"No, seriously. It was the whole reason I came back… to visit the old neighborhood. I never dreamed she still lived there, and when I saw her, I was thrilled."

He was getting ready to respond when Princess let out a yowl, demanding his attention. Shaking his head, he said, "I can't believe she got out and made her way over here. She's an indoor cat but loves to sit in the windowsill. I noticed — too late — the screen in my bedroom window was loose when I was looking for her. She probably saw something in the yard and chased it. Thank God she came over here and didn't wander somewhere else." He bent and scooped Princess up in his arms, cuddling her close as she purred loudly.

Laughing, Bianca smiled benevolently at the pair. "She's obviously yours." She looked around her kitchen and said, "Would you like something to eat or drink? I just moved in, but I did go to the grocery store yesterday."

There was nothing he wanted more than to stay in her presence but said, "Let me run Princess home first, and then I can come back—"

"She's welcome to stay while you're here," Bianca

offered. "I'd hate for you to make the extra trip, and I love cats, so she's fine."

Her lips had curved into a wide smile, and he was overwhelmed with the desire to not leave her side. He lowered the purring cat to the floor, gave her head a rub, then stood and reached out to grab Bianca's hand. Squeezing her fingers, he said, "I want to know everything. Everything about you. Where you've been. What you've done." Looking around, he added, "And how you got *here*!"

Tilting her head to the side, she smiled in return, her gaze never leaving his. "I want to know everything about you, too."

Heart lighter at her admission, he said, "This could take a while."

Her top teeth landed on her bottom lip as another smile slipped out. "Cas, I've got nothing but time."

She turned and walked to her refrigerator, opened the door, and peered inside. She glanced over her shoulder and called out, "Beer, wine, or iced tea?"

"Beer would be good. Any kind."

She grabbed two long-neck bottles, walked over to the counter and popped the tops off. Smiling up at him, she said, "Come on through. The place was furnished, and I haven't added much, but it's comfortable."

He followed her into the living room, and his gaze immediately noted the placement of the furniture. It was not that unusual to place a sofa in front of the window and a wingback chair at an angle facing the fireplace and the sofa. But his gaze dropped to the floor next to the chair where he saw a basket filled with balls of yarn and a couple of knitting needles sticking out. Now he knew why the room seemed familiar… she had replicated Miss Ethel's living room.

She sat down on one end of the sofa, bent her leg and tucked a foot underneath her, twisting her body so that she faced him as he sat down on the sofa as well.

His head nodded toward the basket of yarn, and he said, "I remember Miss Ethel teaching you how to knit. I see you still do it." His eyes drifted to some of the books in the bookcase on the other wall, and he added, "And I see you still like to read." She nodded, and he admired her profile for a long moment, her black hair creating a curtain for her face. "You're just as beautiful as I remember. It's like you haven't changed."

She turned toward him, and he watched as something moved through her blue eyes, something filled with pain. Her smile slipped a little. "There's a lot of things that have changed, Cas. But coming back to this area, I'm hoping to recapture a bit of who I used to be."

Those words did not scare him at all, but instead intrigued him — and gave him hope.

11

Because she had spent time that morning with Miss Ethel, Bianca had been thinking about the past. Glancing over at Cas, she could only imagine how shocked he was. For all she knew, he had spent no time in the last twelve years thinking about her at all. Suddenly nervous, she was clueless where to start.

Looking up at him, she took a long swig of her beer just to give her something to do. He did the same, then his eyes landed on her. He looked different yet so similar. He had grown several inches in height and definitely packed on muscle. Wearing jeans that fit perfectly and ended in heavy, black boots, he had a harder look about him than he did as a teenager. His T-shirt, tight over his muscles, showed the sleeve of tattoos.

His hair, shorter on the sides and slightly longer on top, was a darker blond. A neatly-trimmed short beard covered his jaw and chin. His grey-blue eyes were just as intense as she remembered, and they were scanning her as well.

Self-conscious, she had no idea if what he saw reminded him of the girl he once befriended. Taking another swig of beer, she leaned forward and placed the bottle on the coffee table, the liquid churning in her stomach.

"Nervous?" he asked.

Her gaze shot back to his, and she saw the slight curve of his lips. Nodding, she smiled. "Yeah. It's weird, isn't it? It's been twelve years, and suddenly I can't think of how to begin describing my life."

He leaned forward, placed his bottle on the coffee table next to hers, and suggested, "Why don't you just start talking? You were always so good at expressing yourself."

She thought back to those teenage years when she so readily approached him and began to chat. She had done the same thing with his brothers. Sucking in a deep breath and letting it out slowly, she considered how adulthood puts the kibosh on the easy and open communication of childhood.

He reached over and placed his hand on her arm, his fingertips rubbing gently, and said, "Start at the beginning. Tell me about when you, your dad, and stepmom moved to California."

With her body twisted to face him on the sofa, she propped her elbow on the back cushion and her head in her hand. "I thought we were just going to California because that's where my dad's job was sending him. But he put in for the transfer because Lucille had hounded him about taking a position that would make more money. And her younger brother lived in California and had convinced her that it was the place to be." Sighing, she shook her head in frustration. "So, not only did I get ripped away from you, your brothers, and Miss Ethel, I ended up in a place I didn't like, with a stepmother who didn't like me."

"Your dad put up with her?" Cas asked, surprise in his tone.

Nodding slowly, she closed her eyes for a few seconds, allowing the bitterness to recede. "Yes. I had just started school at the local high school, but by the holidays, Lucille was tired of me being around." She sucked in her lips as her fingers rubbed her forehead, and she held his gaze. "You know, it was only recently that I really, truly understood everything that was happening. At the time, all I knew was that I was definitely not wanted."

Their knees almost touching, Cas settled deeper into the sofa, giving off the vibe that he was in for the long haul. That was something she remembered about him… he was never in a hurry. If she wanted to talk, he listened. Not one person in her life since him would just listen, and a craving deep inside to unburden came forth.

"I'm sure you remember how shocked I was when Dad told me he was getting married because I just thought Lucille was someone he went out with. When I met her, I recognized how very different she was from my mom." She hesitated, gathering her thoughts, then said, "Mom was so laid back, and Lucille was high-maintenance. I didn't know this when I was a child, but my mom's parents were actually very wealthy. My dad was insistent that he did not want her money, so we lived in average houses in average neighborhoods. I know my mom was very easy-going… she had no need for her parents' money. My mom's share of her inheritance was coming to me when I turned twenty-five. Dad had never mentioned that to me when I was younger."

Cas shifted slightly on the sofa, his hand reaching out to hers. She loved his touch, feeling both calmed and exciting at the same time.

"Lucille struck me as being fake from the moment I met her, but my dad seemed happy, so I pushed my feelings to the side and was determined to make the best of things. When we moved to California, we moved into a big house in a gated community. I was surprised but can't say I was unhappy at first. From the moment we landed in California, Lucille acted like she was finally getting the life she deserved."

"What happened?"

"Her brother was much younger than her… he had a different dad, but I thought it might be cool to have an uncle that wasn't a lot older than me since I missed your brothers so much. But I quickly learned he was not to be trusted. He made me really uncomfortable, and when I thwarted his advances, he even tried to slip into my room at night. I told Dad and Lucille, and she accused me of making it all up."

Cas' eyes narrowed as his face hardened. "But your dad… he believed you, right?"

She winced as the painful memories moved through her. "He did but was also willing to accept that Lionel stumbled into the wrong room when he came home drinking."

"Fuckin' hell, Bianca."

The memories made the air feel thin, and she sucked in a ragged breath. "Things became very tense between Dad and Lucille after that. Lucille's dislike of me grew by leaps and bounds. She hated any attention Dad gave me or any money he spent on me. By the holidays, she had convinced my dad that the best place for me was a boarding school. She claimed it had the best education, but what she really wanted was for me to be away from him." Shrugging, she said, "Looking back, I'm surprised she agreed for him to spend the money on boarding school, but that's how desperate she was to not have me around."

"Was that better? To be away from her?" he asked, her fingers now held by his.

Barking out an unladylike snort, Bianca replied, "I transferred to a snooty school halfway through my junior year. I didn't care about fashion and didn't have the latest styles to wear. I loved classical literature and hated modern music. Believe me, I could not have been less of a fit for this school. I managed to make it through the rest of the year because of a wonderful English literature teacher, who I think was thrilled to finally have a student that she could connect with. The plan was for me to go back home for the summer between my junior and senior year, but Lionel was going to be there as well. So, I took summer classes and then rolled straight into my senior year. I had no friends, but at least I wasn't going to be molested."

"I just don't get it, Bianca," Cas said, his expression pained. "How could your dad be so blind? I mean, I know he was gone a lot, but whenever I saw him in the neighborhood, he seemed like a great dad."

She nodded slowly, nibbling on her bottom lip, her mind cast back to days long gone by. Finally, she said, "I don't know how to answer that, Cas. They say love is blind, but in this case, I think love must've been blind, deaf, and dumb. But I have to admit that Lucille was a brilliant manipulator. She could say something that would cut me to the quick and then turn around and sweet talk as soon as Dad walked into the room."

Rubbing her fingers over her chest, she continued, "Soon, everything really went to hell." She looked up and held his gaze, saying, "I used to think her cruel words were stabbing me in the heart, but then, halfway through my senior year of high school, I was hospitalized with real heart pains. It turns out that I had a problem with my aortic valve and had to have heart surgery."

She pulled the top of her T-shirt down a few inches to show the beginnings of the scar that ran down her chest. She watched Cas' gaze lower then jump back up to her face, his eyes wide. His hand slid up her arm and squeezed. "Oh, God, I'm so sorry, babe."

"I missed the rest of my senior year, had to move back home, and was at the mercy of Lucille while I spent months recuperating." Giving her head a little shake, she said, "It sucked."

"Are you okay now?" he asked, his words laced with

concern, and as she stared into his eyes, she could see it was sincere.

"Yeah, I'm good. The surgery was successful. I was out of school for about two months. By that time, my senior year was almost over. Dad hired the English teacher that I liked so well to work with me so that I could finish all the coursework needed to get my diploma. But as far as my health, everything's good."

He rubbed his fingers over the back of her hand, mumbling, "Your fingers are cold. Are you okay?"

She chuckled and said, "I've always had cold hands." Shrugging, she added, "Poor circulation." She turned her hand over and was thrilled when he linked his fingers with hers. It was hard to believe twelve years had passed since she last sat with him, and yet, here they were as adults, still feeling a connection.

"Tell me more," he encouraged. "What happened after you healed?"

"I went to college a semester late, and I found that to get my major and minor it took an extra semester. So, basically, it was five years before I graduated." She closed her eyes and smiled, saying, "Those are my best memories. I was away from Lucille and Lionel, and even though I had to be away from my dad, it was easier. He and I could chat while he was on the road. Or he would come visit me when he was traveling. He still had blinders on when it came to her, but I think it finally dawned on him that she was not all what she presented."

"Is your dad still in California?"

She shook her head slowly from side to side. "No, Cas. He died last year after a long bout with cancer."

Cas' body jerked. "Holy fuckin' shit, Bianca. Your dad marries a bitch who's got a brother you have to try to keep from molesting you. You have open heart surgery and then your dad gets cancer? Jesus, how the hell are you still standing?"

In that moment, Bianca knew what had been missing from her life for the past twelve years. Someone who listened. Someone who believed. Someone who understood. For so many years her father kept believing that Lucille was not as horrible as she was, and it was only near the end of his life that he realized the kind of woman he had married. Before then, Bianca felt as though she had been battling everything by herself with no shield for whatever life was throwing at her.

"I used to think of you," she said, her voice barely above a whisper. His eyes flared, but she continued, "I had no one to shield me. No one to fight for me. It was near the end that Dad finally understood about Lucille, but by then he was too sick to be much of a shield. But even in my darkest times, I used to think of you."

"I should've found you," Cas said, his brow furrowed as he swallowed heavily. "When I got out of the Army, I should've tried to get in touch. I just figured you'd gone on with life. I fucked up."

Leaning forward, she placed her free hand on his leg and squeezed her hand that was still clutching his. "Cas, honey, you didn't fuck up. We were friends as teenagers. We didn't have the maturity or the foresight to try to stay in touch."

"I wrote to you. You'd given me your new address before you left, but I confess I didn't write until I'd already been in the Army for a year."

She reared back, her hand spasming in his. "Wrote… what are you talking about?"

"I figured you had graduated from high school, and I wondered what your plans were--"

"I never got it! I never knew!" A thought hit her, and she lifted her hand to her chest, placing it over her heart. "Oh, God… Lucille. She must have kept it from me." She could not decide if she wanted to scream in anger or cry in heartache. Her eyes searched his. "I wrote to Miss Ethel to find out how you were, but never received a reply."

Eyes wide, he shook his head. "Oh, Bianca… if she got the letter, she would have written back… absolutely."

They were silent for a moment, her mind filled with Lucille's machinations that had managed to keep them apart. He kept her fingers wrapped in his hand, his warmth finally penetrating.

Finally blowing out her breath, she shrugged. "I don't know why I'm surprised. She was… is a horrible person. It seems as though life just happened to both of us. But just the thought of you gave me a mental shield."

The two of them sat quietly for a few more minutes, their attention snagged when Princess strutted into the room, her tail in the air flicking back and forth. The beautiful cat jumped up on the sofa between them and curled up, licking her paws.

Cas turned his gaze back to Bianca and said, "So, how did you escape your evil stepmother's clutches?"

Bianca snorted a laugh, and it felt so good to finally let go of some of her anger. "I never thought about living in a real-life fairy tale, but you're right. She was evil."

"I didn't mean to make light of her."

"You weren't. Honestly, if I didn't sometimes try to find something to smile about, I would have gone crazy."

She released a long sigh. "Dad was diagnosed with cancer about the time that I graduated from college. I worked as an editor, both for a small publishing company and freelance. I also began writing and self-published a couple of books. Dad was still working, even throughout his treatments, until he became too weak. Lionel, who couldn't or wouldn't hold down a job, was living with them, so I didn't move back into their home at first. It took a couple of years, but I began to see some things that concerned me, so I hired a private investigator."

Gasping, Cas leaned forward, his gaze intense. "What did you find out?"

"I found out that Lucille had been married before. In her early twenties, she had married a much older man in Virginia, and when he died, she had a small inheritance. She and Lionel had blown through most of her first husband's money before she even met my dad."

His brow scrunched, he said, "Bianca, did your dad let her know about your inheritance? I don't mean this to sound bad, and your dad was a great guy from what I remember, but it's not like he was... well..."

"The rich husband-catch of the year?"

She watched as he winced, and she gave a little shake of her head. "Don't feel bad. I totally agree with your assessment. My dad was a nice looking, sweet guy. He was a hard worker, a gentleman, and a faithful husband, but to be honest, I couldn't figure out why Lucille went for him because she seemed to like the flashy type. It wasn't until near the end that I started putting two and two together.

"I suppose that when Lucille met Dad, she made certain assumptions about how much he made, and at some point, he must've told her how much money was being held for me. She got her hooks into him, convinced him that she loved him, and figured she had time to get her hands onto the money. What she didn't count on was the close relationship that my dad and I had. He wasn't going to touch that money just to give her or Lionel a better life."

"Did she think that she was going to get it when your dad died?"

She sighed, rubbing her forehead. "Dad was getting weaker, and he and I talked about what would happen if he didn't beat the cancer. I had just come into the money from my grandparents. He also wanted me to know that in his will, Lionel was getting a small amount of money, Lucille would be able to finish paying off her house, and there was a small life insurance policy for her.

"One day, I came by to see him and overheard Lionel

and Lucille arguing. Lionel was mad that she had not gotten Dad to sign everything over to her, including the money set aside for me. She kept assuring Lionel that if she had to forge his name, she was going to get her hands on all the money."

"Fuckin' hell," Cas said again. "I know I keep saying that, but it's the only thing that seems appropriate!"

"I slipped back out of the house so they never noticed me, and that's when I contacted a private investigator and found out that they had no money. I talked to my dad, and I think at the end he finally realized what kind of person he married. He died just a few weeks after that." She held his gaze, squeezed his fingers, and said, "She tried to sue me for the money, and it took months for a judgment to come down, but it did. And in my favor. My dad's will stands as it was written, and the inheritance from my grandparents is all mine. They got none of it."

"I can't believe all you've been through," he said. "And to do it all alone. I wish I'd known. I wish I could've done something."

"You were my shield when I was younger, Cas. You couldn't be my shield forever. Anyway, alone isn't always so bad," she said, her eyes searching his. "I just wrap my good memories around me like a security blanket, and then I can face anything."

12

Cas' mind whirled with all the things that Bianca had told him. He could not believe that everything she had been through had not broken her, and yet, here she sat, staring at him with the same look of happiness that she had when he first met her as an eleven-year-old girl.

As he continued to grapple with the information she had shared, she concluded, "So, here I am. Deciding to come back to a place where I was happy and find out what's next for me."

"How did you get here?"

Laughing, she said, "I drove! I got rid of my small apartment, sold what furniture I had there, let my lawyer and financial planner know what I was doing, and hit the road. I drove north to Washington, then east into Montana. I loved driving for hours and just seeing the beautiful vista, and it was nice to be around so few people after having been in crowded California for so long. I wanted to see mountains, so I came through Wyoming and Colorado. I went through the plains in the middle of the country, and then through Oklahoma and Texas where I walked into the surf of the Gulf."

"Wow… what a trip!" Other than the Army, he had never traveled much, but listening to her talk, he suddenly had the desire to see new places… if he could be with her.

"After that, I came up through the south and then the Great Smoky Mountains in Tennessee and North Carolina. I finally made it into Virginia, which was my destination all along."

Uncertain what to say, he just continued to hold her hand, rubbing her fingers gently as his gaze never left hers.

"Cas, I had no idea you were living next door. I was simply traveling down this road to avoid an accident on the highway when I passed a 'For Rent' sign. I can't explain what made me pull in, but as soon as I saw this little cabin, it was as though all the stress and longing fell away. As though I'd been searching for something for a very long time, and my search was over. I came back to Virginia because I wanted to be in a place where I had once been happier than I've ever been. I had no idea if Miss Ethel was still living in the old house, but I just knew I needed to go by and see."

They sat quietly, still holding hands in the middle of her sofa, the sun sliding behind the trees casting shadows across the front porch. He held her gaze as her hand squeezed his.

She tilted her head slightly to the side, and said, "I've literally just handed you the last twelve years of my life. Please, please, tell me about yours."

He sucked his lips between his teeth and shook his head slowly back and forth. "Bianca, I don't even know what to say. I mean, what you went through... kept going through. I've got nothing that even compares to that."

"This isn't a contest, Cas. We're not competing for who had the worst twelve years. I just want to know about you. The last I saw, you were getting ready to go off into the military and my dad was moving me away."

He stared into her face, seeing earnest interest as she repeated, "I just want to know about you."

He thought back to the last time he had seen her... the goodbye right before they both left Virginia. "The Army was tough. They want to break you down and make your team and your squad become your new family. I get that, but it was a struggle for me at first. I had brothers. I had Miss Ethel. And for four years, I had you. Some people jump straight into that military mindset, opening themselves up and letting others in. Me? It was hard."

"I never thought about that," she confessed. "I know getting through boot camp is hard physically, but I never thought about the emotional aspect." Her eyes dropped to where their hands were clasped. "Did it get better?"

His gaze drifted to the side, his eyes landing on the knitting basket near the chair. "I missed seeing Miss Ethel knit." Seeing her gaze jump back up to his, he offered a rueful grin. "Seriously, everybody talks about being homesick when you're in the military, and honest to God, what made me the most homesick was thinking about her knitting as she sat in the evenings. By the time I joined up and shipped out, Zander, Rafe, Cael, Jaxon, and Jayden had already left home, as you know. That last year, it was just me, Asher, and Zeke." He held her gaze and added, "And you."

Her lips curved and she repeated, "And me."

"You were only finishing your sophomore year and too young for me to go for anything more than friendship. But I admit I liked the idea of you being there when I got out. When your dad jerked you away and took you to California, I figured that was it." He rubbed his thumb over her knuckles and continued, "When we got to our first tour in Afghanistan, I finally realized that people could have more than one tribe. I slowly began opening up to the other members of my squad, learning their stories, learning about their lives, and began sharing about mine."

"Were you stationed in dangerous places?"

Shaking his head, he said, "Shouldn't have been. We were stationed at a base. I was a mechanic. I didn't have a clue what I wanted to do, but Jayden had talked about being a mechanic, and I figured that was always something I could do when I got out. My first couple of tours were okay. Crazy hot summers. Freezing winters. Sand and dust getting in the vehicles, making them run like shit. Sometimes we didn't have the equipment we needed to fix things, so we got good at jury-rigging anything we could. But, by the time I'd been in four years, I was close to my team. I'd found a new sense of brotherhood, a new family. It didn't take the place of my real brothers or Miss Ethel, but I finally felt like I belonged."

"Did you think about getting out?"

Chuckling, he replied, "Yeah, every fuckin' day." Holding her gaze, he said, "But what would I return to? It wasn't until Zander got out and bought Grimm's, Rafe got out and started some crazy-ass modeling career—"

"Modeling?" she all but shouted, eyes wide.

Laughing, he said, "Yeah, Rafe was in some dumbass Army calendar. Ended up with an agent, and as soon as he got out, he was signed. Did that for over a year, living in L.A., until he got sick of it. Came back to Virginia, started work as a landscaper, and met Eleanor."

Joining him in laughter, she said, "I can see that. He was never stuck on himself in high school, but he loved to work out. Even though I was just a kid, I remember thinking he had muscles on top of muscles!"

They sat for a few minutes, their mirth slowly easing back into seriousness. She gave him a silent nudge when she squeezed his fingers again, and he sucked in a deep breath.

"Jayden had just gotten out and was working to buy his garage. He let me know that anytime I wanted to get out, I could come work for him. I was tired of the Army by then but couldn't imagine not being with my team. It may have taken a while, but I'm serious when I said they became my second family. Then the decision was taken away from me."

Cocking her head to the side, she asked, "What happened?"

"We were out one day, having to pick up some equipment that had been blown to shit by an IED. That was the most dangerous part of my job. We couldn't leave anything for the enemy to possibly take and use against us. So, even if something was destroyed, we had to haul it back to base."

He moved his free hand, absentmindedly rubbing it over his chest. "We hit an IED ourselves. Actually two. The first one was in the vehicle in front of me and knocked us to the side. I jumped out and tried to run forward to see who I could save when the vehicle I had been in ran over another one. Blew us all to shit. I landed on my back, a searing pain in my chest. I wanted to get up, but it was as though I couldn't move. I looked down, and swear to God, I had a piece of metal sticking out of my chest."

Her fingers jerked against his as her breath sucked in quickly. "Oh, my God! Oh, Cas!"

"Don't remember much after that. A helicopter ride. Emergency surgery on base. Another seriously drugged-out plane ride to Germany, where I spent some time." With his fingers grasping the neck of his T-shirt, he jerked it down, similar to what she had done earlier, exposing a scar on his chest. "Looks like we're matching, doesn't it?"

They were now sitting very close, and as he stared at her, her eyes never left the puckered scar on his chest. She leaned forward, placing her lips on the top of the scar, giving a little kiss. Her silky black hair was nestled under his neck, and the sweet scent of her shampoo wafted to him. Closing his eyes, a little sigh slipped between his lips.

She leaned back, her eyes boring into his. "You tried to save the others."

"A lot of good it did. We lost several of our team that day, and others were injured." He shrugged, shaking his head slightly.

"So, you came back home."

"Yeah. I convalesced for a little while at Miss Ethel's, then started working at Jayden's garage and reconnected with my brothers."

"And living out here?"

Smiling, he replied, "I got back into my carving and furniture building. I needed more space, so I started looking. Found the cabin and built a workshop almost two years ago. It was perfect. I used some of the money that I'd saved while I was in the Army and bought the place. Up until recently, I was working full-time for Jayden as a mechanic and doing my furniture building on the side. As I started selling a few pieces, especially the ones that have carvings in them, I'm spending a little bit more time doing that."

"I couldn't believe the work when I saw it earlier," she said, her eyes bright. "The pieces are beautiful, Cas."

The shadows had deepened outside as the two sat on the couch. He felt a strange sense of exhaustion from having bared his soul and figured she felt the same. And yet, there was also elation at having reconnected. As he looked toward her, he stared at her profile as she moved her gaze about the room. "What are you thinking?"

Focusing her gaze on him, she smiled. "I've only been back in Virginia for a couple of days, and yet, I feel more at home here than I have anywhere in the past twelve years. I can't believe that I ended up in a cottage right next to the one person I never wanted to say goodbye to and wondered if I would ever see again." Worrying her bottom lip, she asked, "How is that even possible?"

"Agatha Christie once said she noticed when coincidences start happening, they go on happening in the most extraordinary way." Shifting closer until their legs were almost entangled, he whispered, "I'm not going to question it. And I sure as hell am not going to fight it."

He let go of her hands so that he could cup her face, drawing her nearer to him. She came willingly, and he tilted her head slightly so that her mouth was the perfect angle for him to take. Moving slowly to assure that she had plenty of time to withdraw, he was heartened when she closed the distance herself.

Their lips touched lightly, and for a few seconds, he was transported back in time to when his lips touched hers in their first and only kiss. Now, the shackles of childhood were gone, and they both took the kiss deeper. He breathed in her scent as well as the fresh taste of her, his tongue gliding over hers. He swallowed her moan as her body leaned into his. She swung her leg over his lap, straddling his thighs as her hands clung to his shoulders, pulling him closer. Her hair glided over the back of his hand as he held her jaw, the sleek strands every bit as silky as he remembered.

He finally pulled back, sucked in a ragged breath,

and stared at her glossy, kiss swollen lips before lifting his gaze to her eyes, the blue piercing his.

"I dreamed of this," she confessed, her voice a hoarse whisper, and her eyes filled with desire. "For as long as I can remember."

"You're not the only one. I just never thought I'd have another chance with you."

She smiled, and he closed the distance between their lips once more.

13

The kiss continued, flaming hotter with each second. Barely coming up for air, Cas gladly accommodated, letting Bianca rule their movements as the kiss deepened. Her tongue slid inside his mouth, tangling with his, and desire shot through him as she began to grind her soft core against his jean-clad cock.

Her arms clutched his shoulders, and one of his hands slid from cupping her cheek down to grasping her ass. He knew where he wanted this to go, but now that he had her in his arms, he did not want to rush. She was not a woman to bang, but one to be cherished. One to hand the world to.

Suddenly, her stomach growled, and her top teeth landed on her bottom lip. "Sorry," she giggled.

Having lost track of time, he said, "We should eat."

"I'll fix something," she said, starting to move away.

He shook his head. "That's not what I meant. We can go out."

She touched his face gently and smiled. "We're here.

We're talking. We're getting to know each other again. It won't take long for me to fix something, and I'd really like to."

Cooking was not something he enjoyed, and he was not about to turn down a meal. Standing, they linked fingers and he allowed her to lead him into the kitchen. The meal was quick and simple considering she had bought a rotisserie chicken at the grocery store earlier. It did not take her long to make chicken tacos. They tasted amazing even though she kept apologizing that the spice was from a packet that was also store-bought.

Near the end of the meal, Princess yowled loudly, and they both laughed. "Looks like someone else is hungry," he said. He knew he needed to take his cat back home and feed her but hated the idea of being away from Bianca now that they had found each other again.

"I know you need to take her home, but I hate to see you go," she said, staring up at him as she leaned forward to pet Princess.

He chuckled, saying, "I was just thinking the same thing." He loved the way that Bianca said what she was thinking, just like when she was younger. Sighing, he said, "I do need to feed her and make sure my windows are all shut."

They stood at the same time, moving directly into each other's arms. Her head was tucked against his chest, and he felt her soft breath against his arm.

"Um… what are you doing tomorrow?" he asked, hesitation lacing his words.

Her arms tightened around his waist as she leaned her head back and gazed upward. "I work from home, remember? I have some writing and editing to do, but my time is my own." Cocking her head to the side, she asked, "Why?"

"I've got a day off tomorrow, and I thought maybe you'd like to come over. I'll be in my workshop most of the day, so you can come anytime."

Sucking in her lips, she said, "I'd love to. I'd be disappointed if you didn't want to see me."

Letting out a breath of relief, his arms jerked, hugging her tighter. "Honestly? It's all I can do to keep from dragging you back to my house. After discovering each other again and what we just shared, I hate leaving you."

Her lips curved and her smile beamed. "I feel the same. But we don't have to rush this. I'm not going anywhere."

As they walked to her back door, Princess swirled figure eights between their legs. The silence of the night was broken by the crickets chirping, and he felt sure she could hear the pounding of his heart. Once more, as though drawn by a magnet, they stepped closer, her arms encircling his waist as his banded around her back. They stood, their bodies pressed together, wounded hearts now healing, finding peace.

Hours later, he lay in bed, but sleep was elusive. Memories of the past whirled in his mind, slamming into the present, mixed in with a few thoughts of the future. Rolling over in bed, he stared out the window through the woods. Unable to see her cabin, it now seemed unreal that she was truly there.

As she was telling her tale of the past twelve years,

there was so much information to take in, he had not had a chance to process it. But now, in the dark of the night, those thoughts came. *Unhappy home life. Threats from her step-uncle. Heart surgery. Her father's cancer. And then an ugly lawsuit.*

Flipping onto his back, he stared at the ceiling, the last of her story now sinking in. *She has money from her grandparents. A lot of money.* The fact that she was wealthy slithered through him, seeding doubts of them together. I build furniture. I work with my hands. I don't make a lot of money.

Shaking his head in an attempt to dislodge the uncertainty of them creating a future together, he once more tried to find sleep.

Bianca woke early, something she always did out of habit. She stretched in her bed, seeing the dawn just peeking through the slats of the blinds. She thought back to the previous day, for a few minutes wondering if it had all been a dream… Miss Ethel, Princess, Cas.

As she lifted her fingers to her lips, she could still taste him on her tongue and knew that it had not been a dream.

She had been ready to ask him to stay, completely throwing herself at him, when Princess had meowed once more. She had stepped back, watched as he scooped the beautiful white cat in his arms, and with a final kiss, had walked out into the night with promises to see her tomorrow.

She thought that sleep would have been difficult but found that she drifted away easily. In giving her story to Cas, it was as though she had unburdened, allowing peaceful rest to finally come.

Leaping from bed, she hurried through her morning routine. Her phone beeped, and she glanced at the screen, already knowing what she would see. Another text from Lionel… another text she would ignore and forward to her lawyer later. Refusing to let him ruin her plans for the day, she quickly dressed.

Once in her kitchen, she whipped up blueberry muffins, glad that she had stocked up on the ingredients. When they were finished, she placed them in a basket. With a travel mug filled with coffee, she made her way through the woods to Cas' house.

Knowing he would be at work early, she was not surprised to hear noise coming from the workshop. Stepping through the doorway, she spied his body, bent over as he smoothed another coat of stain over the child's headboard.

He looked up, saw her, and his smile split his face. She beamed in return and called out, "I come bearing gifts. Coffee and muffins."

He finished the strokes of his paintbrush, then walked over, placing a sweet kiss on her lips before snagging a treat. They sat in silence for a few minutes, sipping coffee and munching on the muffins.

Swallowing her last bite, she said, "Tell me about your furniture."

His gaze drifted over the pieces in his workshop,

and he shrugged. "I always liked working with my hands."

She laughed and said, "I remember. You were carving a piece of wood the first time I ever saw you."

"It's something I love to do. Something my father taught me."

"I know you probably enjoy working with Jayden, but if this is something you truly love, why don't you do this full-time?"

His lips tightened for a few seconds before he finally sighed. "I'm just learning about the business as I go. It was never something I was going to do as my work, and let's face it, bills have to be paid. Miss Ethel's old dining room table was getting too small for our ever-growing family. Between my brothers finding women and a couple of them already having children, the room is large enough, but the table was too small. I took a look at it one day and decided that I could make a matching leaf to go into the middle. I found the right wood, stained it to match, and even dented it a bit so that it would look like all the dents we ended up putting in the table as we were growing up."

Laughing, she said, "I remember that."

"When I got it in, everybody loved it. That's when Jayden told me I should start trying to make furniture instead of work as a car mechanic. I was afraid to take that chance for a long time, but now the furniture building business is starting to bring in money."

"Are you taking commissioned pieces or just building some and then seeing what sells?"

"I'm still trying to figure it all out. I made a bed for

Zander's daughter, Charity, and carved a princess into the headboard. Then I did a Hansel and Gretel headboard for Rafe's son, Rory. Both of them had friends who saw the beds and have put in orders. That's one of them over there," he said, pointing to the finished bed, "and this one just needs to have the stain dry and it'll be ready."

Grinning widely, Bianca exclaimed, "Sleeping Beauty!"

"So, I do have a few people who are starting to request certain pieces. The difficulty is also deciding the price to put on them."

"I'm sure you can sell these for probably a lot more money than you were thinking," she said. "People love handcrafted items, can recognize quality, and are willing to pay for it."

"Regina told me that I should set up a website, but I'm not sure about that. It's not like I can produce a lot of furniture at one time."

She scrunched her nose and asked, "Regina?"

"That's Cael's wife." Chuckling, he said, "With seven sisters-in-law or almost-sisters-in-law, you'll have a lot of new names to learn."

She nodded and said, "Miss Ethel told me that she wanted me to come for one of your gatherings. I was hesitant, not really knowing what to expect, but now that you and I've reconnected, I'm excited about it."

He stepped closer, bent, and took her lips in a kiss. Barely leaning back, he asked, "Reconnected? Is that what we call it?"

Giving his shoulder a little push, she grinned. "You know what I mean."

He kissed her again before moving over and snagging another muffin. Between bites, he said, "I'm trying to figure out the best way to sell the furniture I make. I've gone to some markets, but I don't want a middleman taking away any of the profits."

Nodding, Bianca said, "I know about self-promotion since I publish my own books and do editing for other authors. You could certainly have a website with some of your designs on it but not have any order form. Someone would need to put in a request and give their contact information and then the two of you could talk about what they like to have. You'd be able to set your price based on what they want, and no one is really ordering until you know exactly what you're building. You can also let them know how many weeks or months it might be before they would get their piece."

His lips curved into a smile, and he nodded. "That might just work."

Before she had a chance to say anything else, her phone pinged another incoming message, and with a quick glance, she silenced her phone and shoved it back into her pocket. Looking up, she saw Cas' head tilted to the side and his brows lowered.

"What's wrong, babe?" he asked. "Who was that message from?"

Throwing off a half-hearted shrug, she said, "No one important."

"The look on your face when you turned your phone off makes me concerned," he pressed. Walking toward her, he reached his hand out and cupped her face, his thumb soothing over her cheek. The feel of him was so comforting, she leaned her head into his palm, closing her eyes for just a few seconds. "Babe?"

Her eyes jerked open and she saw his face, filled with concern, bent low to hers. Sighing, she said, "It's Lionel. He keeps messaging me." She felt Cas' fingers flex slightly against her jaw and watched as something fierce moved through his eyes. "It's okay. I'll just keep ignoring him until he goes away."

"I don't think ignoring him is the best thing to do," he said. "A definite *'Leave me alone'* message should be given."

"Oh, I've given it," she assured. "So, now I'll just let him get tired of sending messages. I don't open them. I don't read them."

Stepping closer, he cupped her face now with both hands, his fingertips in her soft hair, and tilted her head back, lowering his until their lips were a whisper apart. "You've been alone for so long," he breathed. "No more."

He kissed her, his lips moving slowly over hers. The kiss created a slow burn in her belly, one that did not flame out of control but instead sent warmth to every part of her body. She melted against him, and the realization that she was no longer fighting on her own but had someone willing to step in and shield her heart had her fingers clutching his shoulders.

He separated, and she languidly opened her eyes, seeing his smiling face so near. "I want to spend the day with you," he said.

"I was just going to do some writing." Shifting her

gaze around his workshop, she spied his large desk. "I could do it here."

Still grinning, he kissed her lightly. "Perfect." He walked back over to her cabin with her, waiting while she grabbed her laptop and a couple of notebooks, placing them in a small bag. He reached out and took it from her, and they wandered hand in hand back through the woods to his workshop.

Soon, with soft music playing in the background, he continued staining the beds he had made, and she sat at his desk, her fingers flying over the keyboard. Watching him work, still feeling his kiss upon her lips, remembering all that he was to her, inspiration struck and the words flowed.

Occasionally, he would look up, their gazes would meet, and she knew she had found a part of her that had been missing for so long.

14

Cas enjoyed each phase of creating furniture, from planning to the finished product. Carving took the most concentration, but today, as his paintbrush moved back and forth over the wood, the light stain bringing out the beautiful grain, he loved what he was making.

Glancing over at Bianca, he smiled as her fingers quickly moved over the keyboard, knowing a story was being born as he observed. What she did was in many ways so much like his own creating. Ideas. Planning. Execution. Refinement. And then a finished product, born of their own imaginings come to life.

As he moved from piece to piece making sure the stain was even, he thought about all she had told him and was awed at her strength. At most of his worst moments, he was surrounded by people who cared. His parents when he was younger, then later, Miss Ethel and his brothers. Once he opened up and allowed new friendships to take place, his military comrades had his back. Even when he was wounded, he was surrounded by those who did everything they could to help him.

His mind drifted to one of the things that Bianca had told him, something that he had pushed to the recesses of his thoughts. Money. While he was happy with the simple life, one that he wanted to share with her, he was filled with uncertainty once more.

She had rented the cabin next door on a whim, but what happened when the month was over and she decided what she wanted to do next? Travel on? Stay in Richmond but move to a larger house? She admitted that she had inherited a great deal of money, and even though they had just found each other again, he wondered where he would fit in her life. For himself, that question was easy. She could move in with him this very day and he would be happy

Stepping back several feet, he slid his gaze over the furniture, pleased with the warm stain of the wood. His phone vibrated in his pocket, and he pulled it out. A smile moved over his face as he read the message.

"Something must be good," she said.

Looking up, he found her smiling at him, her head slightly tilted to the side in question. "It's Miss Ethel. I sent her a message last night that just said I had met my neighbor."

Laughing, her eyes bright, she said, "I'm surprised she hasn't sent a message to me too!"

Walking closer to her, he said, "Maybe she did, but your phone has been turned off."

Blinking as he approached, she exclaimed. "Oh, my goodness… you're right."

She pulled her phone out of her pocket, and a sweet smile spread over her face. "She did! She also said that she was glad I met my neighbor."

"I can't wait to have everyone meet you again."

He watched as she clapped her hands in glee, beaming at the idea that they would spend the afternoon with Miss Ethel and the whole family. Seeing the smile on her face and her eyes glowing as they held his gaze, he pushed thoughts of her money to the side, determined to fit into her life in any way that she wanted.

"You hungry?"

Nodding, she said, "I'm sorry. I spent way too much time here this morning—"

Throwing his hands up, he stepped closer. "Hey! That wasn't a hint for you to leave. I was planning on fixing something simple for us to eat, and I'd love to show you my house."

Eyes widening, she grinned. "Absolutely, I'd love that." She saved the document she was working on and closed her laptop. Standing, she reached for his hand that was held out for her, and they walked out of the workshop.

The back of his house held a wide, deep deck, decorated with comfortable furniture and a huge grill. Moving through the sliding glass door, they entered the kitchen and she gasped.

"Wow! This is nice!" Turning to him, she asked, "Did you do all of this?"

Shaking his head, he said, "All my brothers helped. Cael and Asher did the design work, and all of us pitched in." She had just discovered the beautiful oak kitchen cabinets with carvings of dogwood flowers along the bottom edge.

"You did these," she breathed almost reverently.

It was hard not to puff his chest out in pride at her obvious admiration "Yeah, that was my idea. I've actually done several for both Cael and Asher's reconstructions. I did it for them as payback for helping me on this place, but both have put in a few orders for homes that they're working on."

She wandered around the kitchen, seeming to ignore the stainless appliances, focusing instead on his woodwork as her fingers trailed lightly over the carvings. Seeing her appreciation, he wanted to show her more. "Come on. There's more to see."

He led her past the dining room, pausing long enough for her to squeal in delight at the handcrafted dining room table and chairs. They moved to the living room that was more of a great room, a stone fireplace at one end and deep-cushioned, comfortable furniture facing a large, flat-screened TV mounted on the wall. She immediately went to the built-in bookcases, her fingers lovingly touching the spines of the books he had collected and read.

A memory struck him, seeing her sitting in Miss Ethel's living room, dusting off books as she discovered each one. "Do you remember the first time you were in Miss Ethel's house?" he asked.

She turned and looked at him, unable to keep the giggle from slipping between her lips. "I know what you're thinking about. When I was dusting off her books on that rainy day when I came over to see if you wanted to play." Shaking her head back and forth slowly, she blew out her breath in a puff. "God, I was such a dork."

"You were never a dork."

Rolling her eyes, she said, "Cas, I was an eleven-year-old girl who asked a thirteen-year-old boy to come out and play. If that's not the epitome of a dork, I don't know what is! I'm surprised you didn't kick me out immediately."

Stepping even closer until he was directly in front of her, he reached out and cupped her face and whispered, "You weren't a dork. Let's just say you were ahead of your time." Without giving her a chance to argue in return, he bent and kissed her, loving the feel of her melting into his body.

When he pulled back slightly, he stared down at her closed eyes, watching as she blinked them slowly open as though waking from a peaceful dream. "Do you want to see upstairs?" His lips continued moving gently against hers. "Specifically, my bedroom?"

Her breath left her in a warm rush over his, and she nodded. "Oh, yeah, I thought you'd never ask."

Taking her hand in his, they linked fingers and he led her up to his bedroom. At the doorway, they turned and faced each other, standing slightly apart. She stared into his eyes and he knew he was drowning. Drowning in memories of what he had hoped would be waiting for him when he returned from the military… drowning in the idea of worshiping her body right now… drowning in hopes for the future.

As though sensing his hesitation, she pulled back slightly and continued to hold his gaze. With a slight separation between their bodies, she reached down and grabbed the bottom of her shirt, gliding it slowly upward while keeping her eyes on his.

If she was waiting for him to stop her, the sight of her exposed pale skin threw out any of his hesitation. The material snagged on her breasts, and she continued to draw it upward until it cleared her head and landed on the floor next to them.

His gaze landed on the scar bisecting her chest, the dark pink line marking the surgery on her heart. He leaned forward and kissed the top of her scar, gently moving his lips along the slightly puckered skin.

She sucked in a quick breath and he lifted his lips, smiling into her face. His arms banded tightly around her back, and he pressed her forward until their lips met once again. Taking over the kiss, he angled his head as he plunged his tongue inside, memorizing the feel and taste of her.

Forcing his thoughts to come from the head on his shoulders, he mumbled, "I don't want to make any assumptions. You've had enough people make decisions for you. I only want to do what you want."

She leaned back and her eyes twinkled. With a slight curving of her lips, she whispered in return, "I'm right where I want to be. I'm doing what I never thought I'd have the chance to do with you… truly, the only man I've ever wanted to be with."

He shifted forward, and her hips stayed pressed

against his as she clasped her legs around his waist. He stood with her in his arms and carried her to the bed.

As he slowly lowered her feet to the floor, she grabbed the bottom of his T-shirt and tugged it upward, exposing his tattoos and the scars on his chest. His chest was covered in angel wings coming from a heart, his scars bisecting off-center. The words *I Had Wings* written in script were at the top of his chest. His arms were covered in tattoo sleeves and words were written on his side. He watched her gaze move over his tattoos before landing back on his eyes. His hands moved to the front clasp of her bra, and with a quick flip, it fell behind her.

He palmed her breasts, flicking his thumbs over her hard nipples before drawing her closer, their naked chests pressed together as he kissed her once again. His hand fisted in the long, silky strands of her hair, holding her close and angling her head as he devoured her lips in a hard, demanding kiss. His tongue moved over hers and he swallowed her moan.

She began to squirm, and he knew she was seeking friction, sure that if he slid his hands down her pants, he would find her slick with need.

Cas moved his fingers to his pants, unzipping them quickly before he jerked them down. While he pulled off his boots and socks before kicking his jeans to the side, she quickly peeled off her pants, sliding her panties down.

His body was on fire with need, and from the look in her eyes, she felt the same. His erection free, he palmed himself as she turned and jerked the coverlet to the foot of the bed. She bent, her perfect ass tilted into the air facing him.

What little blood was left in the rest of his body rushed to his already erect cock as his gaze locked on her ass. She flipped around onto her back, propped up with her forearms by her side on the mattress. His gaze moved from her face down to her sex and back up again, settling on her breasts. She was a gift, and he was awed and humbled at her desire for him.

Putting a knee to the bed, he crawled over her body, bending to suck one rosy-tipped, hard nipple deeply into his mouth. She fell all the way to her back, taking him with her as her fingers clutched his shoulders. Moving between her breasts, he suckled, laved, and nipped. One hand slid between her legs, entering her slick folds. She was so primed and ready, her hips began to undulate as he finger-fucked her while still sucking on her breasts.

Her fingers dug into his shoulders, the slight sting of her fingernails only making his cock harder. He felt her inner muscles clench, and she cried out his name as her release shook her body. Slowly dragging his fingers out, he lifted his head, peered down at her, and sucked her juices from his hand. He memorized the taste of her on his tongue, wanting to never forget this moment.

Her body appeared sated, but as her gaze watched his fingers move in and out of his mouth, she shot up, flipping him to his back, straddling his hips. His hands moved to her ass, and he kneaded the perfect globes as her hair created a dark curtain around them when she bent to kiss him. Knowing she would taste herself on his tongue, he was not surprised when her moans intensified, and her core began to rub against his aching cock.

A groan slipped from his lips, but she must have heard the agonized tone because she leaned up, her brow scrunched, staring at him.

"Fuck, Bianca, I don't have a condom with me."

She sat straddling him, her eyes working as her teeth nibbled her bottom lip. "I'm on the pill, and I'm clean. I haven't been with anyone in… well… a couple of years."

He could only imagine that with everything she had dealt with — her dad, stepmother, and stepbrother — she had not found anyone to be with, she had often been lonely. As much as he hated that for her, he could not help but choke down a roar that he would be the first to give her pleasure and own her body after a long drought.

"I'm not a monk, babe, but neither am I a dog. I haven't had sex in months, and I've always gone wrapped. I had a physical six weeks ago, and I can show you the results. Got 'em on my phone."

"You'd never lie to me."

He held her gaze, her words scoring through him. She gave them freely, no hesitation. She was right… he would never lie to her, but her trust hit him in his heart. "Damn right," he claimed, his voice raspy with emotion.

Her lips curved, slowly at first until she was full-on smiling, and she lifted her hips until his cock was at her entrance. His hands clutched her hips, and his fingers dug into her ass. Letting her control the movement, he broke out in a sweat, his need pulling at him.

She slowly lowered her body, sheathing him as her sex accommodated his erection. Watching her carefully, he noted a slight wince cross her face, soon replaced with a look of pure pleasure. He wanted to plunge to the hilt, thrust to ease the need, howl with desire. Holding on by a thread, he sucked in a deep breath, letting it out only when she had lowered so that she was fully seated.

Bent forward, her hair once more falling in a black silk curtain, she began to move up and down, finding her rhythm, and he knew he had found Nirvana. She alternated between slow and fast, rocking as her breasts bounced.

When she seemed to tire, he took over, thrilled to have given her control but now desperate to give what she needed and take what he could not wait to have. With a quick flip, she landed underneath him, and with his weight resting on his forearms, he began to thrust fully, reaching as deep as he could inside her warmth.

Her legs wrapped around his waist, her heels digging into his muscular ass, urging him on. Not needing the encouragement, he nonetheless loved her enthusiasm. His chest brushed against her nipples, and he memorized the expression on her face… wonder, pleasure, happiness.

As their bodies came together, he leaned down and captured her mouth, his tongue emulating the movement of his cock. Her warmth enveloped him as the friction built. He knew he was about to come but wanted her to come with him. Grinding his pelvis against her clit, he elicited delicious moans from her as she writhed beneath him. Her inner walls began to tighten around his cock, and she threw her head back, crying out his name for the second time.

Feeling the heat roar through him with his final thrusts, he powered through his release. Dots of light appeared behind his eyelids, and he panted, unable to suck enough oxygen into his lungs. Her arms and legs continued to clutch him tightly until he slowed his movements, barely moving to the side as his arms gave out from underneath him. Side-by-side, heartbeats pounding together, legs tangled, they lay for a long time. Neither spoke, and he was sure that he had no coherent thoughts as he continued to breathe in everything that was Bianca.

As their bodies finally cooled, he lifted his hand, threaded his fingers through her hair, and brushed it away from her face. Leaning closer, he kissed her lightly, then grabbed the blanket, jerking it up to cover their bodies. They lay, staring silently at each other for a moment, their warm gazes and soft smiles saying everything.

"I still remember the first time I saw you," she whispered. "You were sitting under some trees. I had never seen anyone whittle before and didn't know what you were doing. But when you looked up at me, even though I was only eleven, I thought you were the prettiest boy I had ever seen. I can't believe you didn't tell me to just get lost."

"Truthfully? I thought about it, but there was something about you that made me answer your questions and talk to you. I don't know, just something about you pulled me in. I figured as soon as you told your father that there were eight teenage boys living across the street, he'd warn you away."

"I think as soon as my dad met Miss Ethel, he felt that I'd always be safe there. And I was."

"None of us would've ever let anything happen to you."

"I know. When I was there, I always felt like I had seven big brothers. Seven brothers and one hero just for me."

He sighed and swept her hair from her forehead. "Babe, I'm no hero. I'm just a man."

She cupped his jaw, her thumb gliding over his stubble, and whispered, "Cas, to me, you're the hero of my heart."

The air hung heavy between them, the long-ago past mingling with the here and now. Her gaze drifted over his chest and arms, and she trailed her finger over the ink. "Tell me about your tattoos… tell me their meaning."

He watched her finger as it moved over his skin, the heat from the single digit searing his blood. Licking his lips, he glanced to his left arm and shoulder, saying, "This is a tribute to my fellow soldiers… my brothers in arms." He tried to see his tattoos through her eyes, hoping that she could understand their significance. "This arm has Miss Ethel's roses, a tribute to my family… both my parents and the family she gave me when I was alone."

She raised up on one arm and trailed her fingers over the words on his side, reading them. A gasp left her lips as her gaze jumped to his face. "Oh, my God... your poems. I remember this one. It was about your family. Oh, Cas, I loved this one."

He swallowed past the lump in his throat as she stared back, tears forming in her eyes. 'I can't believe you remember it."

The air, still thick with emotion, clung to them. "I remember everything, Cas. Everything."

He rolled her underneath his body again, cradling his hips between her thighs, and she encircled his waist with her legs, once more accommodating his body into hers. He felt it and prayed she did too... pouring his feelings into their lovemaking.

Later, once more sated, he cradled her close.

15

Cas woke an hour later, immediately aware of the warm body in his bed, not surprised they had fallen asleep. Smiling, with the scent of Bianca's floral shampoo filling his senses, he pulled her in tighter.

He thought back to their joining, the memory better than anything he could have imagined. So focused on each other, they existed in their own little world as they had made love.

She stirred, her eyes opening slowly, a smile spreading across her lips as she sat up. Kissing her lightly, he said, "I still need to feed you."

As they rose from his bed, she looked around and exclaimed over his boring bedroom furniture. "I can't believe you haven't put some of your own creations in here!"

He shrugged. "This has just been a place to sleep. I haven't had a reason to put anything special in this room." He watched as she bent to grab her clothes from the floor, appearing to be comfortable in her nudity which he loved. Averting his eyes as she dressed to keep from wanting to throw her back onto the bed, he jerked on his boxers and jeans.

Once dressed, he gave her a tour of the rest of the upstairs. The master bedroom contained a large en suite bathroom, with double sinks and a glass block shower as well as a soaking tub. The hallway led to three more bedrooms and another large bathroom.

Peeking in each room, she said, "This place is huge." Turning to him, a curious glint in her eyes, she stated, "This is a house for a family."

He looked at her and his voice caught in his throat. "I didn't want to keep moving around. I knew I wanted to be in the country, so when I was ready to buy a place, I wanted to buy one that was big enough, fix it up the way I wanted, and then one day, when I had a family, I wouldn't have to move."

"You wanted what your parents had," she said softly, her expression gentle as she reached out and held his hand. Her gaze drifted around the rooms, and she nibbled on her bottom lip as thoughts moved behind her eyes.

He wondered what she was thinking but remained quiet, giving her a chance for her thoughts to flow.

"Did you… um… build it with someone in mind?"

He heard the tentative tone in her voice and shook his head. "There's never been anyone special for me. I've dated but never any one person for very long. I suppose, as soon as I could tell there was no long-term possibility, I ended it."

She turned and faced him fully, still nibbling on her lip. “How could you tell?”

He thought about the few women he had dated, only two for any length of time. “I dated one woman for a few months, but she didn’t care for the creative process of woodworking. She became increasingly irritated at the amount of time that it took away from her. Being a mechanic was okay because I came home at the same time each day and then could focus solely on her.” Lifting his heavy shoulders in a shrug, he said, “I get it. I really did—”

“No,” Bianca exclaimed, her hair moving with her head as she shook it back and forth. “She would never have been right for you. Your creative desire just bubbles from deep inside. To try to keep you from your woodworking and carving would be like telling a painter that they can’t paint.”

“Or telling a writer that they can’t write,” he added, his lips curving.

“Exactly!” Her penetrating gaze hit his face. “Was there anyone else?”

“There was only one other woman that I saw for several months, but she didn’t enjoy reading. I mean, that’s cool, but any time I would mention something that I was reading, she would roll her eyes and claim that it was boring.”

Eyes wide, Bianca shook her head again. “You’re so much better off without them.”

They walked slowly down the stairs, hands still clasped together, and at the bottom, they stood in the hallway between the great room and the dining room. A sigh slipped between her lips, and she asked, "What did they think of your house?"

Stepping closer, he said, "They were never here. I bought this place after them. I knew that if I built the home the way I wanted it, that would also help me know when I found the right woman. It would be someone who understood me."

Blinking as though in surprise, she said, "But this place is beautiful! It's perfect and I don't see how any woman would not like it."

He lifted their hands that were clasped and placed hers over his heart, pressing her fingertips to his skin. Lost in her gaze, he smiled. "That's what I was looking for. Someone who felt the same way about it as I do. A house in the woods, big enough for a family, waiting to be filled with love."

He watched as she sucked in her lips. Her eyes searched his for a few seconds, filling with something undefinable before darting away.

Moving into the kitchen, they worked side by side, fixing a simple meal with Princess wandering between their legs. As they sat down and began eating, he asked the question that had been on his mind. Swallowing, he asked, "What about you? Anyone special?" As the words left his mouth, he realized how vulnerable they made him feel, which in turn made him realize that she had just put herself out there for him when she had asked the same question.

He could not help but breathe a sigh of relief as her head slowly shook back and forth.

"I didn't date in high school," she admitted, "mostly

because it was an all-girls high school. I simply never had the opportunity to meet anyone. Lionel and Lucille had done a number on my self-esteem, so I wasn't exactly putting myself out there, either. The idea of ridicule was overwhelming. So, I spent most of my time in my head, creating the characters in my life that I wanted to be with, then putting them down on paper."

His heart ached for the lonely teenager that she described, and he reached out his hand and gently squeezed her fingers. "What did they do?"

Her gaze drifted out the window and she sighed. "Lucille was so needy… she had to be the center of attention, and if she did not get it, then she was just plain mean. I swear, I think her mirror was her best friend, as much time as she spent in front of it! She had to be the most beautiful, and to make sure she felt that way, she constantly told me I was too skinny, or my complexion was splotchy, or my hair was limp. She encouraged me to dress in drab, ill-fitting clothes. She said it was so that I would not draw undue attention to myself since I was so *unfortunate looking*, but I think it was just because she did not want any competition."

Shaking his head, he wished he had Lucille in front of him now to let her know exactly how he felt about her cruel words said to Bianca.

"And Lionel? After he was… um… rebuffed by me, he also joined in with the ugly taunts." She looked at him and added, "I know you're wondering why I didn't talk to Dad about this." Shrugging, she said, "He traveled so much, and when he was home, I just wanted him to be happy."

Continuing, she said, "Then I got sick, and to be honest, for a long time I thought little of anything but getting better. I admit that college was my chance to spread my wings. I attended some college parties, met some guys, finally lost my virginity… or rather, I should say I chose to give it away. He was a nice guy, but even then, I knew it was not forever. I didn't go crazy in college, but I certainly realized that was the first time I felt like I was experiencing life since I had been in California."

"I'm glad you had that," he said. "Everyone should have a chance to experience some life out on their own, even when they're young and foolish."

She nodded her agreement. "When I got out, Dad was sick, and I had little time to experience anything other than helping him and all the emotions that swirled inside."

"It's weird. I want to say that I'm sorry you never met anyone special or had anyone to share your life with, but then I'm also selfish to say that I'm glad. If you had, you wouldn't be sitting here with me right now."

She smiled, linked fingers with his, then finished eating in companionable silence. The afternoon passed similarly to the morning… she working on her manuscript, and he on his furniture.

"I need to run back to my house and grab one of my notebooks."

Cas looked up at Bianca as she tossed a smile and

wave toward him before leaving the workshop. Two days had passed, and they had spent every moment together except when he was at the garage the previous day. But their nights had been spent together.

Now, the next day, they were back in his workshop. He was glad that he had been staining and was not sure how she could have worked with the louder machinery. So far, she had stayed perched on a table in the front corner by a window, near the open door, her fingers typing a steady rhythm on her laptop.

Taking the opportunity to cut a few pieces of wood while she was gone, he then looked up at the sawdust floating through the air. *Damn! Her laptop!* He grabbed the vacuum and hustled over to the table. Pleased that it looked as though there was little sawdust on the table, he quickly vacuumed over and around her laptop and phone. Turning off the vacuum, he picked up her phone to move it away from the edge of the table. Almost on cue, it chimed several times in a row, indicating texts coming in, one right after the other.

He knew he should look away, and yet, at the screen right in front of him, he stared at the gray text bubbles, reading each word.

Hey, babe. Miss you. Did you get my message?

Can't wait to see you again.

As soon as I can get to you, I'll come.

You and me, together... Always.

There was no picture of the sender at the top of the screen, just a letter. **B.** He dropped the phone onto the table next to her laptop and stepped back. He knew he should not have looked and hated that he did so, but what had been seen could not be unseen. His chest deflated as air rushed from his lungs, the reality of her situation slamming against the words she had spoken.

She had never expected to see me again. Her plans of just seeing her childhood home may have altered with discovering me, but that doesn't take away the fact that she has someone. Someone waiting for her. Or rather, someone who plans on joining her here.

Scrubbing his hand over his face, he fought to catch his breath. Nothing made sense. He could hear her humming as she reapproached the workshop and darted away from her laptop and phone, making sure to be standing next to the piece of furniture he had been working on. He tossed down the rag and tried to force a smile onto his face as she stepped to the doorway.

"Got it!" She held a spiral notebook in her hand, clutching it to her heart as though it were treasure.

"I… uh… hate to cut this short, but I got a call while you were gone. I need to go… uh… go to the garage. I'm needed there. So… uh…"

"Oh, sure." She tilted her head slightly, peering at him as though to discern a possible mood change. He remained silent, and she turned toward the table, picking up her laptop and phone before sliding them along with the notebook into a bag. "I'm sorry you have to go into the garage today. I know you'd hoped to finish what you're working on."

"Yeah, well, the paycheck from the garage pays my bills." A flash of surprise moved through her eyes, and he silently cursed his harsh tone. Still feeling as though he could not suck in enough air, he turned away from her as he closed and locked the workshop door. Not knowing what else to say, he forced another smile onto his face and said, "I'll give you a call."

She stepped forward and placed her hand on his chest, lifting on her toes for a kiss. He acquiesced, loving the feel of her lips on his, but quickly stepped back. "Hate to run, but Jayden's in a real pickle without me." Again, he ignored the hurt that had replaced the surprise on her face.

"Oh, well, okay. Just give me a call and I can come back over anytime. Or you can come to me… I'm just through the woods." She winked, and her lighthearted tone drew him in, but before he had a chance to change his mind, she offered him a smile as she tossed her hand up in a wave.

He hustled through his back door, standing away from the window while still peering out as she walked slowly away from him and into the woods toward her house. Placing his hands on his hips, he dropped his chin and slowly shook his head. He felt like an ass for practically shoving her away from him, and yet, the texts were burned into his mind. *Fuckin' hell. Now what do I do?*

16

Two days. It had been two days since Cas walked out of the workshop, sending her on her way. Bianca stood in her kitchen, caught between fuming and wanting to cry. When he did not call the night he left, she assumed he must have gotten in late. She knew the next day was a regularly scheduled day for him to work in the garage, but again at night, no word from him.

She had walked through the woods and knocked on his back door, but there was no answer. His pickup truck was not parked near the house, but she was unable to see inside the garage, so she had no idea if it was in there.

Now, it was the morning of the third day and he had not contacted her. It was as though he flipped a switch on their relationship. Put the brakes on. Called a halt. All the other idioms she could think of ran through her mind, but they all meant the same thing. For some reason, Cas decided that he did not want to be with her.

Swallowing deeply, that idea cut through her. *After*

all we've been through. After finding each other again. After all we said to each other. Why?

It was that last 'why' that had the fury storming through her. If he did not want to be with her it would hurt, but she had dealt with hurt before. But to walk away without giving her a reason, to stop what was building without giving her the courtesy of an explanation — that had her pissed.

She slammed her coffee mug onto the counter with such force, she was surprised it did not shatter. Sliding her feet into tennis shoes, she darted out the back door and stomped through the woods. Coming out on the other side, she noticed the door of his workshop was standing open. *So, he is home today! Home... and didn't bother to contact me.*

Reaching the open doorway, her feet stuttered to a halt as she saw him standing in the workshop, his back to her, his head bowed. A beam of sunlight was coming through the window, illuminating him, and her angry words fled. Just as she was about to call out, he began speaking, and she realized he had his phone pressed to his ear.

"You're not telling me anything I don't know. I know I shouldn't have looked at someone's phone messages, but they were right in front of me and I did."

He paused, probably listening to the person on the other end of the line, but Bianca was more focused on the words he had just said. *Is he talking about me?*

"Why should I try to talk to someone when I don't know if they're telling the truth? Sure, I thought it was something special, and then I saw messages from another guy. Messages that indicate she's still in an ongoing relationship."

She stared at his back as he still faced away from her. Her mind raced, wondering who he could be talking about. *An old girlfriend? Or someone he was seeing right before I moved in? But he told me there wasn't anyone.*

"No, no, it isn't anyone you know. Just some girl who moved into the cabin next door."

At those words, she gasped, eyes wide in disbelief. He whirled around at the sound, his eyes growing wide as they locked onto hers.

"Shit, I gotta go." His hand fell to his side, his phone dangling in his fingers. "Bianca, I didn't mean for you to hear that—"

"No kidding, asshole." Her entire body vibrated with anger and betrayal. As though moving of their own accord, her feet stomped into the workshop. "I couldn't believe you ignored me for two whole days, and I've made myself sick with worry about what was happening. I replayed every conversation that we had over and over in my mind, and all I could remember was the sharing and the caring and the desire to become something. I memorized the moments we lay naked in each other's arms, and you gave me no indication that I was *just some girl who moved into the cabin next door.*"

Hands lifted to placate, Cas stepped forward, his face anguished. "Jesus, Bianca. I didn't mean it like that. I just... I just haven't had a chance to figure out what to say to you."

Tilting her head to the side, her eyes bugged. "What to say to me? Hmmm... let's see. *'It was fun seeing you again after all these years, and by the way, you're a great fuck?'* Something like that? Or maybe more along the lines of *'Gee, it's not you... it's me.'*"

In the face of her sarcastic anger, his face hardened. "You're hardly the hurt person here, Bianca. I saw the messages from your boyfriend. I know I shouldn't have looked, but they came in on your phone when I was standing right there."

She fell back a step, his words hitting her in the gut, causing her to suck in a quick breath. "Wh… what are you talking about?"

"The messages that came in a couple of days ago. '*Hey, babe. Miss you. I can't wait to see you again. I'm coming. You and me, together... Always.*' From B. Talk about words being burned on my brain! How do you think I felt falling in love with someone only to find out she was playing me?"

The pain that hit Bianca's heart was as powerful as what sent her to the hospital years before. Only this time, she knew it was the pain of a heart that had shattered into a million pieces.

Her feet wanted to turn and run. Her mouth wanted to scream until she was hoarse. Her eyes wanted to weep. But for a moment, she could do none of those. Instead, she stared at the boy she had loved and lost and the man she had wanted a future with. Reality slipped over her, its icy fingers wrapping around her body, and she shivered.

She turned and stumbled to the doorway of the workshop, her hand reaching out to hold onto the doorframe, uncertain her legs would continue to hold her upright. Her fingers tightened against the wood, and she sucked in a deep breath. Looking over her shoulder, she held his gaze. "I told you that Lionel was still trying to contact me. By the time the trial was over, his initial pleas for money had turned to threats, which then turned into declarations of love. I didn't block his number because my lawyer encouraged me to forward all texts to her. She said they would be important if I needed to obtain a restraining order."

She heard him gasp, but she did not give him a chance to speak or come closer. "The *B* was for Lionel *Baxter*. I couldn't stand to see the name Lionel pop up on my phone so often, so I just labeled it as *B*."

"Oh, shit, Bianca. I'm so fuckin' sorry," he cried, rushing toward her.

She threw her hand up to stop him, afraid that if he did, she would not have the strength to do what needed to be done. "Don't touch me!" By now, she was facing forward and had walked several steps into the yard. She could feel his presence hovering nearby, but she tamped down the desire to fall into his arms, afraid that if she turned around fully and stared into his face, she would give in.

Glancing over her shoulder once more, she said, "*Your* number, on the other hand, I *will* block." With that, she raced toward the woods, desperate to find solace in her own little cabin.

The next day, Cas sat in the office of the garage, leaning

forward with his forearms resting on his knees, his eyes staring at his hands. "I can't believe how bad I fucked up." He lifted his gaze and stared at Ruby sitting in her chair, her eyes full of sympathy. He had given her the gist of the story, mentioning that Bianca was somebody he knew from long ago. Jayden was out on a towing assignment, and Cas had taken the opportunity to confide in Ruby.

"Why do you think you were so quick to assume those texts were from a current boyfriend and that she had been lying to you?"

Snorting, he shook his head. "Damn, you go straight to it, don't you?" He saw her lips curve slightly, and he sucked in a deep breath before letting it out slowly. "As excited as I was to see her and be reunited, I guess deep down inside I couldn't believe that she really wanted to be with me. She's smart and beautiful. She works for herself, editing and writing books. On top of that, she's got family money. She used to live in a gated community and went to a private school. I'm... I'm just... not that."

"And what are you?" Ruby prodded.

He held up his hands and said, "I work with these. No matter how much I scrub, I think grease is embedded. These nicks and cuts come from the tools I use in my woodworking. I wear jeans and boots, not suits. My house is surrounded by trees, away from most other people, which is the way I like it, but not many people want a hermit-type life."

"You not only didn't trust her, you didn't trust yourself." Ruby leaned forward, her eyes radiating understanding. "Cas, I was just like you. I cleaned fancy houses for just enough money to cover my expenses. Then, at the end of the day, I went back to my grandmother's tiny house. When the man I was dating was mean, it was sometimes hard to believe that I deserved better. When Jaden came into my life, I thought he was too good for me. He was smart, owned his own business, had people in his life that adored him." Lifting her thin shoulders, she shrugged. "I was just plain old Ruby. It wasn't that I was unhappy with my life, I just couldn't believe that he wanted to share his life with me."

Nodding, Cas silently agreed, her words resonating. "I was so stupid, Ruby. She's been through so much. If anyone deserves to not be hurt, it's her." He winced, remembering the pain on Bianca's face when he last saw her. "I don't even know how to start fixing what I broke. Maybe I can't. Maybe I should just stay out of her life and leave her to something better."

"And if you do?"

His head jerked up and he stared at Ruby.

She continued, "And if you stay out of her life, how does that make you feel?"

The idea that he would never see her again after having found her sliced through him. "I have to believe it was fate that brought us together the first time. Fate that brought us together last week. I don't want to lose her again."

Ruby smiled. "Then tell her you're sorry. Ask for forgiveness." She laughed, then added, "Remember what Benjamin Franklin said… 'Never ruin an apology with an excuse.'"

"Oh, great," he complained. "Are you saying I shouldn't try to explain what I was thinking?"

Shaking her head, Ruby said, "You can explain your reason, but Cas, don't try to pass it off with excuses. Just be honest. Just be you."

"What if it's not enough?" He swallowed deeply, his chest tight.

"Then you'll know. You'll know if she's truly the right one."

They sat in silence for a moment, then they heard the rumble of the large tow truck as it pulled in front of the bays. Standing, he said, "Thanks, Ruby. I'll follow your advice and pray that she forgives me."

Just as he walked out the door, she called out. "You know, a grand gesture also goes a long way." Laughing, she winked as he rolled his eyes.

17

Bianca stared at the open document on her laptop, but no words came. Writing romance always came naturally. For years it was what she dreamed of, and she would weave tales based on those dreams. Then, for a few glorious days, she finally understood the way the heart truly beat in time with another person.

Leaning back in her chair, she glanced out the window. *A few glorious days.* Even to her own ears that now sounded foolish. No one in real life can fall in love in a few glorious days. *But it wasn't just a few days... it began years ago.* She rubbed her forehead in an effort to still the ache in her head.

The weather had been so mild, she loved having her windows open to allow a breeze to blow through. Suddenly, she sat up straight, cocking her head to the side. The sound of tinkling wind chimes met her ears. She had not remembered hearing that before. She jumped from her seat and walked toward the back door, curious to see where the lyrical sound was coming from.

There, hanging from a tree in the back yard, was a beautiful wind chime. Hurrying outside, she gasped as she recognized the handiwork. The top was a round disc of smooth, stained wood, the image of a tree carved in relief. From around the outer edge hung strings, each connected to a beautiful colored piece of glass. As the breeze blew, the chimes rang out a delicate melody.

Nearby, hanging from another branch, was a piece of paper. She reached up and snagged it, her breath catching in her throat as she unfolded the page and read it aloud with the sound of the chimes in the background.

"I am so sorry for hurting you. I could inflict all kinds of pain on myself, but it would not take back any I gave to you. Maeve Binchy"

Her breath left her lungs in a rush as she held the paper against her chest. She recognized the quote from one of her beloved books, *Echoes* by Maeve Binchy. It was the first book she had borrowed from Miss Ethel and had always thought that David's apology was beautiful.

She was uncertain how to respond. His gesture was so beautiful, and yet her disappointment had been so great she was reticent to move forward. Inwardly growling, she wondered why all the great emotions had to clash… love and anger, heartache and redemption, pride and forgiveness.

Battling the urge to run straight to see him, she walked back into the house, laying the sweet note on the kitchen counter. After fixing a cup of tea, she sipped the hot brew, allowing her churning emotions a chance to settle. From the front of the house, she could hear a slight knocking. Unable to keep from leaping to her feet, she rushed to the front door and threw it open.

There was no one there, and disappointment scored through her. Being honest with herself, she had to admit she had hoped Cas would be standing there. The slight knocking could still be heard, and she stepped forward, looking to the right of the porch. There, much to her amazement, sat a beautifully carved rocking chair. She had seen it in Cas' workshop, unfinished in the corner.

She darted to it, her hand lovingly gliding over the smooth wood. The curved top of the chair back was carved with the same little boy and girl peeking from behind the tree that Cas had used in the baby beds. Another note was tucked between the slats of the seat. Snatching it up, she unfolded the paper, her eyes eager to see what he had written, not surprised to see another quote.

"I can see no lightness, no humor, no joke to make. I just hope that we will be able to go back to when we had laughter, and the world was colored, not black and white and gray. Maeve Binchy"

As before, she held the note to her chest, only this time tears hit her eyes. Refusing his apologies was pointless when her heart sang to be with him. She rushed inside, sliding her feet into her sneakers. Racing out the back door, she ran through the woods, not stopping until she rushed into his clearing. There, sitting in the middle of the yard, was a beautiful wooden chest, another piece that she had seen in his workshop.

Approaching it slowly, she took in the intricate carvings. She recognized Snow White being led into the woods, holding the hand of the Huntsman as he guarded her heart. Tears slid down her cheeks as she carefully lifted the lid, hoping for and finding another note. Her hands shook as her eyes devoured the words.

"I'll understand if you don't want me, but I will be heartbroken. You were all I ever dreamed of and hoped for. You are much, much more. Maeve Binchy"

Lifting her gaze, she stared as Cas stepped from his back door, a bouquet of flowers in his hand. His eyes roved over her, fear in them as though he was afraid she would disappear. He hurried forward, and she met him in the middle of the yard. They stopped awkwardly a foot apart.

Before she had a chance to speak, he rushed, "I am so sorry, Bianca. I can't believe how horribly wrong I acted. Everything. Everything I did was wrong. I should have never looked at your phone when I moved it. I should've never read those messages. I should've never jumped to conclusions that were so stupid to begin with."

She kept her gaze on his face but could see the flowers in his hand shaking. "Why did you?"

Anguish moved across his face as he winced, shaking his head quickly. "It was me I doubted. When we were kids, it felt like we were equals. Both having suffered loss. Both looking for friendship. Both connecting with someone that others might consider a little different."

Remaining quiet, her lips quirked slightly at the reminder of them as children. He, sitting under the tree whittling while she twirled about the yard.

"But now, twelve years later, we've led vastly different lives. I began to doubt that I was someone you would want to settle for. When I saw those messages, I gave in to my doubt. It made me realize that in our excitement of being reunited, we haven't had the time to figure out exactly who we are and what we want as a couple." His chest heaved as he peered deeply into her face. "What you overheard was me talking to Jayden. The reason I said you were just a girl who moved in was I couldn't bring myself to admit that you had come back into my life and I had fucked it up so badly. I don't know what else to do but beg your forgiveness. Wherever we go from here and whatever we become, at least I need to know that you—"

"I forgive you." Tears stung her eyes as the words rushed from her, and she watched him blink before his eyes narrowed slightly in uncertainty. She stepped closer until the only thing between them were the flowers touching both of their chests. "I was miserable without you. I thought about it, replayed the scene over and over in my mind. Yes, you jumped to conclusions and did not give me an opportunity to explain, but I also reacted the way I've learned to do. Walk away. Pull into myself. Separate myself from whatever has upset me."

She reached out and took the flowers from his hand, sniffing their scent and admiring their beauty before holding them to the side so that she could step closer.

With her head leaned back so she could continue to hold his gaze, she said, "If we're going to make this work, then you need to move past the doubt that I want to be with you. And I need to learn to stand and fight for what I want."

He lifted his hands and gently slid his fingers through her hair as his palms cupped her cheeks. Bending, he kissed her ever so lightly. It was the barest hint of a kiss, but she felt all of the emotion it offered. Regret and sorrow. Forgiveness and redemption.

As he started to pull away, she let the flowers fall gently to the ground as she reached up and grabbed his shoulders, holding him in place. Lifting on her toes, she kissed him fully, not willing to let him go. His arms banded around her back as he pulled her tightly to him. This kiss was different as their lips moved together and their tongues tangled. This was a kiss of letting go of doubt and embracing new beginnings.

18

Sitting in his truck as they rumbled down the road, Bianca swiped her hands over her sundress in an attempt to smooth out the wrinkles and remove the nervous dampness from her palms. Still needing something to do with her hands, she fiddled with the strap of her purse.

She jumped when Cas reached his hand over and placed it on her leg and realized she had been bouncing her knee up and down the whole time.

"Are you nervous?" he asked.

Looking over at him, she rolled her eyes and shot back, "Wouldn't you be?"

"Sweetheart, it's your family. You've always been family."

"I can't believe everyone's getting together just to see me again."

"Babe, you're a surprise."

She swung around to look at him, the silky screen of her hair swinging out with the movement of her head.

Her blue eyes, impossibly wide, stared at him. "Surprise?" she squeaked.

"When Miss Ethel calls, everybody comes. Whether there's a reason or not. So, she asked if everyone could come today because she had someone she wanted them to meet."

"Oh, my God, now I'm more nervous! Everyone is giving up a Saturday afternoon to reunite with a dorky teenage girl they used to know years ago." She dropped her chin to her chest, her hands coming up to cover her face.

"Don't be nervous! They're going to be so excited to see you again. So excited to see us together."

Her hands fell into her lap and she looked over at him again. A slow smile curved her lips, and she asked, "Together?"

His brow furrowed and he shot her a hard stare. "After what we just shared for the past couple of days, I would think *together* is the right word. Is it not?"

At that moment she could not think of a word she loved hearing more from his lips than *together*. Not just sitting in his truck together at the same time. Not just neighbors that together shared a few meals. Not just a random hookup together. But two people who actually wanted to share their lives… that kind of *together*. Still wanting to make sure she understood what he was saying, she murmured, "We haven't exactly defined anything."

Turning off of the main road, he slowed, then parked and turned off the engine. "Then let me make myself perfectly clear. I haven't just been playing house with you for the past few days. I can't predict the future, but based on our past, I'd say we're starting to build something special. Something that I want to keep building." His gaze stayed pinned on her long enough to watch her face soften, and he added, "And I hope that's what you want, too."

He leaned toward her, and she shifted so that she could meet him in the middle. They kissed, long and sweet. He slid his tongue inside her warmth, and she felt tingles move through her. Separating slightly, she murmured, "That's what I want, too."

"Good," he said, shifting back in his seat. Reaching down, he adjusted his crotch and said, "Give me a minute, babe. I don't want to walk in with my cock leading the way."

Her forehead crinkled at his words, then she turned to look out her window and realized they were parked on the street outside Miss Ethel's house. This time, the driveway was filled with trucks and SUVs. She sucked in a quick breath, willing her nerves to settle. *It's just old friends.* As Cas opened her door and held out his hand to assist her down, she smiled. *No, it's just family.*

He kept her hand tightly grasped in his as they walked toward the front porch, her excitement at seeing everyone beginning to overpower the nerves. Before they reached the front door, they could hear the sounds of laughter coming from the back yard. He turned to walk around the house with her in tow.

Once they reached the back corner, he said, "You ready?"

Sucking in a deep breath, she let it out slowly, then smiled. "As ready as I'll ever be."

He leaned forward and kissed her soundly, sweeping his tongue inside her mouth. Her knees felt weak, the way they always did when he kissed her.

Grinning, he winked. "Let's go."

As they turned the back corner of the house, she could see that Miss Ethel's back yard had changed little over the years. There was more grass growing, no doubt due to the lack of ball games with eight boys continually stomping on the lawn. A tree she remembered in the back yard was even larger, its branches covering two picnic tables pushed together.

The sight of seven large men and eight women had her feet stumbling to a halt.

Miss Ethel saw them coming and clapped her hands. "Here's Cas, and he brought an old friend of ours."

She stood rooted to the spot as everyone's eyes swung around to them. She could tell that Cas was still grinning widely as he propelled them forward. As she got closer, she could easily discern each of the boys, now men. Zander, with his deep-set eyes intensely searching hers and a toddler in his arms. Rafe, just as handsome as always, a toddler held close to his chest. Cael, still towering over the others, his shock of red hair more of a deep russet than when he was younger. Jaxon and Jayden with their long hair pulled back, and she had to admit she could not instantly tell them apart. Asher, tall and lean, his discerning eyes moving over her. And Zeke, also with long flowing hair, head tilted slightly to the side, a smile playing about his lips.

My seven dwarfs... my seven giants.

In the slow-motion of dominoes falling, one by one, their eyes widened and their mouths dropped open in recognition. Suddenly, tears pricked her eyes as the years fell away, and she again felt like the lonely preteen who was looking for acceptance. Swallowing audibly, she felt Cas pull her back against his chest, his arms encircling her.

He whispered, "It's okay, babe. You're home."

The men rushed forward, all exclaiming her name at the same time. Pulled from Cas' arms, she was hugged by each of them, questions filling the air as well as heartfelt greetings.

Overwhelmed, she wiped the tears falling from her eyes as she returned hugs and laughed with the joy that was filling her.

19

Bianca could not remember the last time she had laughed so much, enjoyed herself so much, or eaten so much.

After having reunited with the men, each of them introduced her to their wives or fiancées. Trying to remember everyone's name, she quickly figured them out, finding them to be as unique and united as the men.

She had been plied with questions until Miss Ethel finally threw her hands up to quiet everyone. "I suggest we let Bianca tell her story as she would like."

Not wanting to belabor any of her depressing story, she gave them a basic rundown of her life after she moved to California. Their emotions appeared to run the same gamut that Cas' had... horror at Lionel, anger at Lucille, concern over her health, and sorrow for the passing of her dad. But, ultimately, joy that she had decided to come back east, followed by shock that she had so easily met up with Cas again.

Once the introduction and tales of the past were over, they settled around the picnic tables laden with food. Miss Ethel and the women had outdone themselves. Her delicious fried chicken was surrounded by bowls of potato salad, fruit salad, broccoli and cheese casserole, baked beans, and fluffy homemade rolls, followed by cake and pies.

They finally moved to a large circle of chairs surrounding an unlit fire pit. Zander, keeping an eye on his daughter, asked, "What are your plans now?"

Sitting next to Cas, comforted by his fingers linked through hers, she replied, "To be honest, that's rather open-ended." She felt Cas' head turn toward her and knew his gaze was penetrating. She gave his fingers a squeeze and explained, "What's happened in the past several days is more than I ever expected or hoped for." She heard his audible sigh and continued, "As I told you, when I left California, I wanted to see a lot of the country and spent almost two weeks driving through places that I had only read about. At each place I visited, I asked myself the question, 'Can I see myself living here?' I saw so many beautiful places, and yet, I wanted my journey to bring me back here. To see it, if nothing else, for one last time." Smiling, she looked over and caught Miss Ethel's twinkling gaze and said, "I had no idea that you'd still be here."

Laughing, Miss Ethel said, "And I told her that there was nowhere else I'd rather be. This house may be large, and I don't go upstairs very often, but with the help of my sweet boys, and now all of my girls, I'm able to stay in my home."

"That's wonderful," Bianca said, her voice hitching. She realized with the sound most everyone's eyes jerked back to her, but she shook her head, swallowing deeply. "No, no I'm fine. It's just that discovering that you all are still here and closer than ever makes my heart so happy."

Giving a mental shake, she continued, "But, as far as my plans now, I'm not sure. I don't need the money that was left to me from my mother's family, or even the money from my father. I'm going to invest it for now and can live off of what I earn. Because I work from home, it makes it easy for me to live anywhere. California was never home. And all the places I visited were wonderful but didn't feel like home." She glanced to the side, not wanting to make Cas feel uneasy, and just said, "I guess I'll see what happens."

Without hesitation, Cas said, "If I have anything to do with it, you'll stay. This is home. With all of us. With Miss Ethel. With me."

She whipped her head around as he slid his arm around her shoulders. Tears filled her eyes once again, and she was caught by surprise when he leaned forward and kissed her lightly in front of everyone.

Looking up, she could not help but notice the huge smiles of the women who were also snuggled against their men. Glancing toward Miss Ethel, Bianca saw that her smile was the widest of all.

After a while, they began moving around, the women

gathering Bianca into their fold as the brothers moved to the side to talk.

Zeke clapped Cas on the back and said, "I can't believe Bianca's here after all this time."

Rafe shook his head and said, "I mean, damn, I was just talking about her not too long ago."

"Do you think she'll stay?" Zander asked, his gaze moving from Cas over to where Rosalie was chatting with Bianca.

Cas' gaze had rarely left Bianca, and he said, "I hope so. I have to admit we jumped into a relationship right off the bat. It may seem quick, but it was years in the making."

"Hey, the rest of us will tell you that when you know, you know. When it's right, it's right," Jaxon said.

Jayden grinned, adding, "I guess you didn't get a lot of work done after finding out she was your neighbor."

Shaking his head, he said, "That's what was so cool. We spent a lot of time getting to know each other, but then I'd be in the workshop working on the furniture, and she would take her computer out and work there as well. I thought it might be too distracting for her, but she seemed to get a lot of writing done."

"Can you see it working?" Cael asked. "Long term?"

"Honestly?" he replied, holding Cael's gaze, "The four years that she lived here, I fell for her. I never said anything, but I was going to tell her that I was coming back for her when I got out of the military. But right when I graduated from high school and was ready to go, that's when her dad and stepmom hauled her off to

California. It's been twelve years, and I thought it was long over, but I never forgot her."

"When you think of it that way," Asher said, "then it's really not something very new. Kind of like rediscovering someone you knew a long time ago. A lot like me and Penny."

Nodding, he said, "Yeah, you're right. It is a lot like that."

The sound of women's laughter reached them, and the men looked over. The eight women were surrounding Miss Ethel, their smiles filled with true joy.

"Do you know how fuckin' lucky we are?" Zander asked. "Given my early years, I would not have thought I could've had a family like this."

Cas knew exactly what Zander meant, and he did not have to look at his brothers to know that each one of them understood as well. Their backgrounds were diverse, but one thing bound them together: each had found themselves as children needing to be placed in a foster home. Being placed with Miss Ethel was the greatest thing that could have happened to them. She had brought them together and made them a family and was now bringing into the fold the women that they had chosen for mates.

He knew that Bianca had been worried earlier as they drove to Miss Ethel's, but he was certain she would fit right in with the men that she remembered from years ago, and with Miss Ethel, who had given her a mother figure during her teen years. And now, he watched as she stood with the other women, her head thrown back in laughter, her silky black tresses flowing behind her.

How was it possible that he had watched each of his brothers find love and now she had walked back into his life? *Love? Could it possibly be love so soon?* He told his brothers that it was like a renewal, not just something new. Looking back at her, his smile widened as he acknowledged he never wanted her to leave again.

Bianca had been excited about seeing Miss Ethel again, but the idea that the men would have forgotten all about her and that their women would not like her had made her a bundle of nerves. But she should not have been worried. The men were as welcoming as long-lost friends, and their women seemed eager to include her in their sisterhood.

"I couldn't imagine who you were when you walked up," Regina said. "But the way the guys reacted, I knew you were someone special."

She smiled at the statuesque redhead. "I was really nervous coming over here. I had no idea if any of them would remember me, although I admit I was a constant pest when I was younger."

"Oh, my dear, you were never a pest," Miss Ethel said.

Rolling her eyes, she laughed. "The first time I came over, I met Cas as he was sitting under a tree, whittling. He was thirteen years old, and I asked if he wanted to play with me. Then I heard his brothers in the back yard shouting, and he told me he had seven brothers. Somehow, I imagined they were much younger, and I told him it would be like living with the seven dwarfs. He didn't correct me, and then the next day when I came over and met everybody, I called them the seven giants."

The other women burst into laughter, and Rosalie exclaimed, "That's so funny. I'll have to call Zander my little dwarf the next time he gets on my nerves."

"Oh, please, don't. I don't want him to hate me."

"I don't think you have to worry about that. Like Regina said, the way all the guys reacted when they realized who you were, you're definitely like their long-lost sister," Eleanor said.

Cas had told her a little about each of them, and she was amazed at their stories. Tales of bravery, overcoming obstacles, triumphs, and independence.

She discovered that Morgan was the Olympic swimmer who had an accident and had reconstructive surgery and rehabilitation on her arm. Rosalie had suffered a brain injury and spent time in the hospital not remembering who she was. Eleanor had suffered severe burns when she was a nurse in the military and had undergone agonizing hospital stays, surgeries, and rehabilitation. Regina was a cancer survivor. Even Penny had been involved in a car accident as a child and suffered greatly through multiple surgeries and treatments.

She found camaraderie with Ruby when she heard that she had been in an abusive relationship and also with Cynthia's experiences with her own stepmother.

The women talked and laughed, and Miss Ethel

promised to share her fried chicken recipe with Bianca as long as she shared a few of her knitting patterns in return. As the others were chatting, she felt her phone vibrate in her pocket. She ignored it for a while, then, when she could do so discreetly, she pulled it out of her pocket, glanced at it, jabbed a few buttons, and shoved it back into her pocket. Glancing over at Cas, she found his eyes pinned on her.

"Is everything okay?" Rosalie asked.

Nodding, she forced a smile and said, "Sure. No problems."

"I hope I'm not overstepping my bounds," Ruby said, "but Cas is looking over here like he'd like to rip your phone into pieces. Are you sure nothing's going on?"

Having already mentioned Lucille and Lionel when talking about her time in California, she sighed and said, "It's now been over a month since the judgment was handed down, and I'm afraid that for the past week, Lionel has been sending me texts saying that he'd like to talk to me. I've tried ignoring them, but that doesn't seem to work."

"Perhaps you should talk to Cas about it," Penny suggested.

She shook her head. "He knows, but it's my problem, and I'll handle it. The last thing I want to do is drag Cas into something unsavory."

"Well, take it from us, our men are super sweet but definitely alpha. I don't think Cas would be very happy to find out that this is an ongoing problem," Morgan advised.

"I'll think about it, but I'd still rather just handle it myself."

As she was talking, she noticed Rosalie's eyes growing wider, but it was not until she heard a voice directly behind her that she realized why.

"What's the problem?"

Hearing Cas' growl behind her, she whirled around. Placing her hands on her hips, she said, "You shouldn't sneak up on people!"

By then, the other men had moved back to the group of women and she could feel all eyes on her. Heaving another sigh, she said, "Just another message from Lionel." Looking at the others, she said, "For the past week, Lionel's been sending me messages. He says he wants to meet with me, but I told him that I have nothing to say to him. Since then, I've been ignoring his messages."

"I told you that it's time for someone else to get the message across to him," Cas said, and she blinked in surprise at him as the other men's heads nodded in agreement.

She placed her hand on his arm and said, "Not now, Cas. We're having a lovely evening, and I don't want it ruined."

He wrapped his arms around her and kissed her forehead. "I'll give in for now, but if he keeps bothering you, I want to know."

"I can handle it myself, you know," she argued while whispering.

He kissed her once more. "I know. But I can have your back while you do it."

Smiling, she had to admit that sounded good. It had been a long time since anyone had her back. Leaning into him, she melted into his embrace as they continued to enjoy the rest of their evening.

20

The weeks flew by. Weeks of absolute bliss. When Cas was working at the garage, Bianca spent her days in her cabin, the words flowing as she worked on her next book. When he had a day at home, she took her laptop to his workshop and found that his creative process with the wood seemed to spark her creativity as well.

She had already had lunch several times with the women and visited with Miss Ethel, showing her the knitting patterns she used to create her blankets.

It was hard to believe that two months ago she was still embroiled in the fallout from her father's will and Lucille's attempt to get more money. Lionel's texts had stopped, and for the first time in many years, she felt as though she could breathe freely.

She and Cas spent their nights in his house, Princess keeping them company, curled up at the foot of the bed. The realtor had contacted her to see if she was going to renew her lease for another month, and she readily agreed. Cas had questioned if she needed a place separate from his, but she had not wanted to crowd him. Plus, the small cabin gave her a place to spread out and use as an office.

Today dawned bright and sunny, and Cas had gone into work at the garage, having finished two more beds and a table that he had been working on. She had relished the long goodbye kiss he had given her, excited that each morning started that way.

She was so close to the end of her manuscript that she hoped to get it finished soon but also had several errands she needed to run. Stepping out onto her back patio with her morning cup of coffee, she could not believe how her life was finally turning around. She only hated that her father was not here to see what was happening. She knew that if he had not gotten sick, she would have come back to Virginia after college. But would she and Cas have gotten together then? Maybe they still needed more years of life experiences before they would have been ready for the relationship that they now so quickly jumped into.

Bianca's phone rang, and she did not recognize the number. She had all of the women now programmed into her phone but answered it anyway. "Hello?"

"Bianca? Please don't hang up!"

She recognized Lionel's voice, and her thumb hovered over the disconnect button. She thought about what Cas had said, but the last thing she wanted was for him to get in trouble for threatening Lionel. Squeezing her eyes tightly shut, she willed away the nerves shooting through her and moved her thumb. "Lionel, we don't have anything to say to each other. By continually trying to get hold of me, this is considered harassment. I don't understand why you can't get it through your head that when I left California, I left everyone *from* California as well."

"I know, I know. I'm not trying to harass you, but I just cannot get it out of my mind how everything went so wrong."

Not understanding his words, she repeated, "Everything went so wrong? I don't know what you're talking about."

"I know now that taking you to court was wrong. I admit that I listened to Lucille and initially wanted part of your inheritance. She always told me I would get more from your father. Looking back, I realize I've foolishly allowed Lucille to lead everything... for most of my life. That was weak, and I know it. Since the time the judge blasted us on the day he threw out the suit, I've taken a hard look at what she's been doing. I'm afraid if I don't make changes, it's going to ruin my life."

"Ruin *your* life?" Furious at his words, she could not understand why he was calling or what he wanted.

"Please let me explain," he begged. "I discovered that Lucille has been using my phone to send messages to you. Obviously, it looked like they were coming from me. She thought she was erasing them or deleting them... hell, I don't know what she was thinking. I'm not stupid, Bianca, although I've done a lot of stupid things in my life. Since that day you left California, I told Lucille I was done with her. Done with her machinations. I've got a job interview coming up... away from California and away from Lucille. It's only a low-level entry job that a friend helped me get. The last thing I need is any trouble with the police, so I got a new phone and canceled the old one to keep her from doing that again. I just needed to let you know."

His anguish sounded sincere, but not being able to see his face made her doubt. She was quiet for a moment, then sighed. "Okay, if you're just calling to apologize, then that's fine, and we have nothing further to talk about."

"I'd really like it if we could meet—"

"Oh, no!"

"Please, hear me out, Bianca. I'm here in Virginia. I came to the East Coast for the interview, but also because I just want to see you to apologize in person. I know you don't want to be alone with me, so we could meet in public. There's a restaurant in the hotel where I'm staying. It's big, well lit, with lots of people around. You'd be perfectly safe to meet me here. I need to get on with my life, Bianca. My life away from Lucille. But I need to do it starting off with the apology to you. Please, let me do this."

She sighed heavily, not wanting to have this conversation with him. She could easily see how Lionel, practically raised by Lucille, had his ideas about money and lack of work ethic indoctrinated from his sister. It was so hard to decide if his words were true, but before she had a chance to answer, he continued.

"I need to learn to stand on my own. I need to learn to be my own man. Hell, I need to learn how to be a man. I knew it on that day we walked out of the courtroom that I wasn't who I wanted to be. I told Lucille that I didn't want to see her again. I never got the chance to be the kind of man your father wanted me to be while he was still alive."

Bianca closed her eyes and thought of her father and how often he had sat and talked with Lionel, hoping to teach him how to stand on his own. Maybe, just maybe, her father's lessons were taking hold. "Okay, I'll meet you, but only in public, and only for coffee. What hotel are you at?"

"The Belvedere. It's pretty old, but the rates were good. I've been to the restaurant, and it looks very nice."

"I'll be there at two o'clock this afternoon."

She heard the relief in Lionel's voice. "Thank you, Bianca. Thank you so much."

"Don't make me regret this, Lionel."

Hours later, she parked down the street from the Belvedere and sat in her car for a few minutes. She had sent Cas a message to let him know where she was and what she was doing. He often did not have a chance to check his phone when he was working on a car, and so far had not sent a return text. Climbing from her vehicle, she walked toward the hotel. It was an old brick hotel in downtown Richmond that had probably seen better days, but the tall first-floor windows and stately doorman in the front gave it an elegant feel of times gone by.

Once inside, she walked briskly to the restaurant that was at the front of the hotel. The hostess smiled at her and she glanced around, seeing Lionel sitting at a table for two near the front windows. He was dressed in slacks and a polo shirt, his hair neatly combed. He had always been handsome, and she often thought that if he was not so influenced by Lucille, he might have been a good catch for someone... *but not me!* An air of nervousness surrounded him as he fiddled with the stem of his water glass.

She indicated to the hostess that she was meeting someone and headed to the table. Halfway there, he looked up and saw her, a hesitant smile on his face. He stood quickly as she approached and reached his hand out to shake, then pulled it back as though uncertain if she would want to have contact with him.

She walked to her seat and he hustled around to hold her chair for her. As soon as she was seated, a server came to ask what she would like to drink. Seeing the goblet of water on the table and glad that Lionel had no alcohol present, she murmured that coffee was fine.

"Are you sure?" he asked. "Would you like something to eat?"

Shaking her head, she said, "No, I don't think so. The water and coffee will be enough."

Feeling the need to do something with her hands, she picked up the water goblet and sipped while waiting for her coffee. Her attention was snagged for a few minutes as a rather large and noisy party seated near them was getting ready to leave. She was glad for the distraction, not having to stare at Lionel, waiting to see what he would say.

The server came, bringing their steaming cups of coffee and placing a plate of small scones in front of them. After fixing her coffee, she focused her attention on him and said, "I have to admit I'm very surprised you came to Virginia to see me."

"It was a risk, I know. And I had even prepared myself for your complete rebuttal. But I felt strongly that I wanted to have a chance to talk to you."

As they ate the buttered scones, he began, "I don't have an excuse for any of my past behavior, but I have come to see reason. As you know, Lucille was fifteen years older than I was, and by the time I was five, she was practically raising me. Father was nonexistent, and her mother spent more time nursing her vodka than taking care of me. Lucille found every way she could to snag a man that would take care of us. When I was younger, I didn't think anything about it. It was simply the norm. She wanted a better life and had no idea how to get it other than finding a man who would take care of us."

Not having anything to say to his confession, she simply nodded for him to continue.

"I don't even think your father knew this, but he was her third husband."

At that, Bianca's eyes jerked wide open. She had no idea Lucille had been married twice before her father. That was something her private detective had missed. If her father had known, he had never mentioned it to her.

As Lionel continued to talk, she tried to stifle a yawn. She caught his questioning gaze and apologized. "I'm so sorry. I'm suddenly so very sleepy." She lifted her hand to her forehead and gently rubbed, adding, "I think perhaps I should leave. I truly accept your apology, and you can certainly go on about your life without worrying about me." As she spoke, Lionel's face became slightly out of focus.

"Bianca, I don't think you should drive," he said. "Not if you're not feeling well."

She yawned widely again, and said, "Perhaps you're right. I could call for a taxi."

Lionel called the server over and gave him a credit card to pay for their lunch. After signing, he hurried around to Bianca's chair and assisted her to her feet, saying, "Come on. Let's walk around some and see if you feel better. If not, is there someone I can call?"

She allowed herself to be assisted from the chair, and Lionel banded his arm tightly around her waist as they walked out of the restaurant. Her vision was still blurry, and her brain felt fuzzy.

"Walking is probably helping," she mumbled. With her hand in her purse, she tried to pull out her phone, continuing to mumble. "I'll call Cas…"

Walking through the lobby, Bianca's legs felt like rubber and she was vaguely aware of being led around, but her tongue felt too thick for her mouth and words did not come. As the elevator doors opened, she tried to remember why she would want to go to the upper floors. "Lionel, no. No elevator."

The truck that Cas had been working on was finally complete. He wiped his sweaty brow and headed into the office to let Ruby know he was finished. Glancing at the clock on the wall, he was not surprised that his stomach was growling, considering it was the middle of the afternoon and he had missed lunch. He went into the break room, scrubbed his hands, and grabbed a water bottle. Pulling out his phone, he sat down at the table with his sandwich, thinking he would call Bianca to see how her day was going.

He saw that he had missed a message from her an hour earlier where she told him that she had decided to meet Lionel at the Belvedere restaurant since he was in town and said he wanted to apologize in person. Leaping to his feet, he cursed, "Shit!"

Jayden, walking into the break room, immediately asked, "What's wrong?"

"Lionel… that guy from California, Lucille's brother, came to town and convinced Bianca to meet him, supposedly so he could apologize in person."

Jayden's head jerked, his brow furrowed. "All those years being a dick, he gets shut out by the court when trying to contest the will, and within a month he suddenly wants to apologize?"

Already peeling out of his coveralls, Cas said, "Yeah, right. I gotta leave, bro. I'm heading to the Belvedere."

"I'm going with you," Jayden said, darting back into the office to give Ruby a quick explanation of where they were going.

Eyes wide, she warned, "Be careful!"

As Cas came tearing out of the break room, Jayden said, "I'm driving."

Not wanting to take the time to argue, Cas tossed his truck keys to Jayden and climbed into the passenger side. Just then, his phone rang, and he looked down to see who was calling. "It's Bianca."

"Hey, sweetie," he greeted. He heard no reply other than what sounded like muffled scratches. "Sweetie? Bianca? Are you there?" As he continued to listen, he shot Jayden a quick look. "Get us there… fast!"

21

Lionel guided Bianca into the elevator and pushed the button for the fourth floor. When the doors opened, Bianca continued to walk down the hall on rubbery legs. Her weight was partially held by Lionel as she leaned heavily on him.

"It's a fun house," she mumbled, then a giggle slipped out from her lips. The memory of her father taking her to the fun house at a carnival when she was a little girl moved through her and she laughed again. Watching the numbers on the doors as they passed, she called out, "Four-thirteen... four-fifteen... four-seventeen... oh!"

Lionel opened the door and guided her into the room. Staggering, she stumbled toward the bed, sinking into the soft mattress as she bent forward and propped her head on her hands.

Wishing the room would stop spinning, she heard a familiar female's voice call out, "How much did you give her?"

Lifting her head, trying to focus, she watched as Lucille stepped from another room. Lucille's head seemed to float away from her body, and another giggle erupted from Bianca's lips. She attempted to point but was uncertain that her hand was moving in the right direction when she slurred, "Whas you doin' here?"

"Jesus, Lionel, can't you do anything right?"

"I did exactly what you told me, Lucille. I put everything in the vial into her water," Lionel argued.

"How much did she drink?" Lucille asked, her fists on her hips.

"She didn't order anything else to drink except coffee, but she ended up drinking all of her water," he continued.

Bianca's gaze bounced back and forth between the two others in the room as they continued to argue back and forth, but the movement made her dizzier. Finally, giving up the attempt to follow their argument, she flopped back onto the bed and closed her eyes. Unfortunately, she continued to feel as though she was in a boat on the waves even with her eyes shut, and her stomach rolled.

"How can we get her to sign these papers if she's unconscious?" Lucille cried out.

Bianca heard the words but struggled to figure out what Lucille was talking about. *Papers? Signed? I signed all the papers my lawyer gave me. I think. Were there more? And why would Lucille want me to sign papers?*

"You can't do anything right, can you?" Lucille complained, her voice harsh.

"Shut up," Lionel growled in return. "I got her to meet. I got her to drink. I got her up here. I did my part. You've done nothing but bitch and moan my whole life about how unfair life is. You bitched your way through three husbands but didn't count on the last one not planning on making you sole heir. So, bitch your way out of that!"

The ping-ponged words bounced around in Bianca's mind, but she found it too difficult to make sense of them. Opening her eyes, she tried to focus her vision on Lucille's pacing and Lionel's angry face. The instinctive desire to be safe kicked in, and she knew she did not want to be in this room with them regardless of what they were arguing about.

Pushing up on her elbows, she licked her lips and sucked in a deep breath before sitting upright. Her head immediately felt like it was rolling and her stomach pitched. She bent forward, her hands on her knees, and gulped in air, forcing her lungs to breathe deeply. She looked up and saw that the door to the hall was only about ten feet in front of her. Blowing out her breath, she managed to get to her feet, but as the room swayed, she was uncertain if it was her unsteady feet or just her swimming head.

"I want her signature on these papers, but they need to at least look like her handwriting," Lucille groused.

"Well, when the effects of the drug start to wear off, then we'll get it," Lionel bit back. "That would be the same as how she would be if she had only drunk a little water."

"Yes, but by then will she be missed?" Lucille bit back.

Bianca took a step toward the door, but Lucille whirled around and grabbed Bianca's arm. "Oh, no, princess, you're not going anywhere."

"This fucking plan is going south," Lionel cried, stomping about the room. "It was never going to work. I can't believe I let you talk me into this!"

"Shut up—"

"Open up! Hotel security!" a deep voice boomed from the other side of the door.

Bianca stumbled as Lucille dragged her into the bathroom, closing the door behind them, her fingernails biting into Bianca's arm.

"Stay in here and stay quiet!" Lucille ordered, and Bianca tripped over to the sink before sliding onto the floor.

Cas and Jayden stood outside room four-seventeen in the Belvedere Hotel, pounding on the door. Calling out, "Hotel Security," he wanted to kick in the door, but Jayden held him back. On the way over, he could hear Bianca's slurred voice calling out hotel room numbers and prayed he was at the right one.

Just as he lifted his hand again, the door opened. A young man, dressed nicely but with a face full of fear, said, "Yes, may I help you?"

Putting his hand on the young man's chest and pushing his way into the room, he looked around.

"You can't come barging in here!" the man shouted.

"What the fuck have you done with Bianca?" Stalking toward the bathroom, he tried the door, but it was locked.

"My wife is in there taking a bath," the man said, starting toward Cas but finding Jayden's hand now planted in his chest.

Calling out, Cas said, "Whoever's in there better get away from the door because I'm coming through."

The lock on the door clicked and he hesitated. The door barely moved, and a woman's face was partially seen through the opening. Lucille. Cas recognized Lucille… older, but definitely her.

"I'm indisposed," Lucille said, her eyes wide.

"Bianca!" he called out.

"Cas?" a weak voice came from within the bathroom. He gave the door a shove and Lucille flew backward, her arms propelling as she tried to regain her balance. His gaze landed on Bianca, now slumped on the floor next to the bathtub. "Call 9-1-1," he yelled to Jayden. "Police and ambulance!"

Leaving Jayden to deal with Lucille and the man he assumed was Lionel, he dropped to the floor, pulling Bianca into his arms. "Baby, baby, talk to me!"

"Casssss," she mumbled, then giggled. "I can't feel my body."

"What did they give you?"

Her head wobbled and he stood, picking her up in his arms, stalking out of the bathroom. Looking at Lucille, whose hard gaze was shooting arrows in his direction, he then turned to Lionel, who appeared as though he wanted to throw up. "What the fuck did you give her?"

"It was her... she gave it to me!" Lionel rushed, pointing toward Lucille.

"Shut up!" Lucille shouted.

The sound of heavy footsteps came from the hall and Jaxon appeared in the doorway. "I'd already called him," Jayden explained as his twin rushed in with his paramedic equipment and partner.

"Let me see her," Jaxon said. "Put her on the bed." As Cas lay her down, he kept her hand in his.

Jaxon immediately began assessing Bianca, asking what she had been given. As the police arrived, Jayden filled them in over Lucille's protestations.

"Rohypnol," Lionel whispered. Clearing his throat, he repeated it. "Rohypnol."

"Roofie? You fuckin' roofied her?" Cas roared, anger bursting forth as he stood from the bed, taking a step toward Lionel.

Jayden quickly stepped in front of him, placed his hands on Cas' shoulders, and said, "Stand down, man. Let Jaxon help her, and let the policemen do what they gotta do."

Lucille made a grab for a sheaf of papers on the table, only to be stopped by one of the policemen. Chaos ensued with Lucille still screaming insults toward Lionel and threats toward the policemen who were in the process of getting them out of the room so that the paramedics could load Bianca onto a gurney.

Forcing his attention back to her, Cas rushed out

with them, calling over his shoulder to Jayden, "Call Detective Chambers... Zander's friend."

Entering the elevator with Jaxon and Bianca, he leaned against the wall as the door closed to the cacophony still coming from the hotel room.

22

Bianca snoozed in the hospital room, slowly coming awake as the sound of soft voices came into focus. Opening her eyes, she saw Cas' face bending over hers, his eyes searching.

"Baby?" he whispered. "You comin' back to me?"

Nodding, she blinked several times. "What happened?"

"Do you remember anything?"

Sucking in her lips as she pondered, she shook her head. "Uh… not really." Her brow scrunched. "Yes, Lionel… I remember Lionel."

Fear snaked through her as she wondered what she was doing in the hospital with Cas looking ready to go ballistic. Her gaze shifted behind him, and she could see the room was filled with his brothers, all with the same expressions that Cas had. "What's everyone doing here?"

Pete Chambers stepped into the room, looking around before moving to Zander and shaking his hand.

"Sorry to have to meet like this again." With chin lifts to the other men, he walked to her bed and said, "Nice to see you awake, Ms. Winters. I'm Detective Chambers."

Shooting her gaze back to Cas, she asked, "What's going on?"

"Babe, you were roofied by Lionel," Cas replied.

Her eyes shot open wide and she struggled to sit up. He put his hand on her back, slid into the bed with her, and supported her as she sat upright, facing the detective.

"Ms. Winters—"

"Bianca, please," she interrupted. "Ms. Winters makes me think of Lucille!"

Nodding, his lips curving slightly, Pete agreed. "Okay, Bianca. The doctors have confirmed that you were given Rohypnol by Lionel Baxter. He obtained the illegal drug through Lucille Winters. In their hotel room, we found an unsigned will from you, listing Lionel and Lucille as your heirs in the event of your death."

Her eyes bugged and she began, "But, I never—"

"Unsigned, babe," Cas said softly, drawing her eyes to him. "They had it ready for you to sign."

Shaking her head, she said, "What were they thinking?"

"Bianca," Detective Chambers said, drawing her attention back to him. "I've spent the past two hours with Lionel and Lucille, and I can tell you that I'm not impressed with either of their abilities to think through a plan. What I can tell you is that while they have not admitted it yet, my guess is that once they had you sign the will, they would take you somewhere to sleep off the drug and then you wouldn't remember anything about it. That's what Rohypnol does... it causes amnesia, along with the confusion and other side effects."

"But they still wouldn't get anything until I had died." Gasping as the words left her mouth, she clutched Cas' arm tightly.

"Yes, ma'am, you're right. What I'm sure Lionel will confess to is that Lucille planned on an accident being arranged at some time in the future that would cause your death, therefore giving them access to your money."

Slumping back against Cas, she felt nauseous. Just then, a doctor stepped into the room and eyed the large gathering.

"Who are all these men?" the doctor questioned sharply.

"They're my friends," she said, her voice stronger. She looked around at Zander, Rafe, Cael, Jaxon, Jayden, Asher, and Zeke and said, "My friends... my giants."

They all chuckled, but the doctor simply shook her head. "Well, if your friends can wait outside, I'll go through your checkout information."

They all shuffled outside, calling out that they would meet up with her and Cas soon. The doctor looked at Cas and lifted her eyebrow.

"Oh, no," Bianca said defiantly. "He stays."

Once the room had cleared, the doctors said, "Rohypnol stays in your system for several hours and then leaves without a trace. It appears that you never completely lost consciousness but suffered the side effects of confusion, drowsiness, lack of muscle control, forgetfulness."

The detective spoke up. "From what Lionel told us, he placed the Rohypnol in your water before you got to the restaurant. He expected you to drink some but order something else to drink. He thought you'd get a little loopy, then he'd easily be able to talk you into going upstairs and signing the papers, and then the effects would wear off. Instead, you drank all your water and therefore had more of the drug in your system."

"A nurse will be in to get you to sign your hospital forms," the doctor said. Her gaze shifted to Cas, sitting at Bianca's back. "A special friend?" the doctor said, a slight smile playing about her lips.

"Yes," she replied, twisting her head around to stare at Cas' handsome face. "A friend… and my shield."

Cas grinned despite his earlier expression of anger and kissed her lightly. Nodding toward the doctor, he pulled Bianca back against his strong body once more.

The drive home was mostly silent, Bianca lost in her thoughts. She knew if her father could see the woman he had married, he would be horrified. And furious. She knew if he could see the young man, one he tried to influence to become a better man, slip something into her drink, he would be devastated. She thought of the seven men — friends — who dropped everything they were doing to rush to the hospital to check on her.

"Cas, how did you know which room I was in?"

"Babe, it was you. You were calling out the room numbers as you walked down the hall with Lionel.

Four-seventeen was the last one you called out. It was a guess, but one that I prayed was right."

Glancing to the side, she smiled at him, thinking of how he raced across town with little to go on other than her initial message and her drugged mumblings over the phone to get to her side.

Turning onto the drive toward Cas' house, she visibly startled when she saw the number of cars, trucks, and SUVs parked in the front yard.

Swinging her head around toward Cas, she asked, "What on earth is going on?" Before he had a chance to answer, his front door opened and his brothers and their women began spilling out onto the front porch. And right in the middle of them was Miss Ethel.

Parking, he turned toward her. "This is family, Bianca. This is what family does. I know you remember it from a long time ago when your mom and dad were both alive, and you haven't had it for many years. But this is us, you and me, and your family now."

Tears slid down her face, but she knew they were tears of joy. Cas opened her door and assisted her down. As her feet settled onto the gravel drive, he bent and kissed her lightly. She wrapped her arms around his neck, pulling him close. "Let's go enjoy family."

He grinned and nodded, but just as he started to step back, she tightened her hold on him and added, "And then we'll work on enjoying ourselves."

He threw his head back in laughter, then bent and scooped her into his arms, walking toward the porch filled with their family.

23

FIVE YEARS LATER

Zander stood by the front door, glancing into the mirror that was hanging by the entranceway, checking his tie. He hated wearing a suit, finding jeans, T-shirts, and boots to be more to his taste. His employees would call that his standard uniform, but to him, once he took off his military uniform for the last time, he was glad to just be comfortable.

He glanced into the living room, seeing Rosalie's efforts in home decor mixed with their kid's toys. Last night she had managed to get all the toys in a basket by the side of the sofa. He had shaken his head and told her not to sweat it. Kids' toys in the house just meant that they had a home. That was more than he ever had growing up before he landed in the foster system.

In fact, he had never owned a toy until he arrived at Miss Ethel's house.

As always, thoughts of her brought a smile to his face and caused his heart to squeeze just a little. How she took a scared boy who had been living out of a dumpster and had never been to school and turned him into the man he hoped he was… there was no way he could ever repay her.

He once asked her, many years ago, what he could ever do in return for all that she had given him. Her soft smile had turned toward him as she lifted her thin hand and patted his cheek.

"My dear boy, being allowed to be your mother has given me more than any riches in the world. Remember, St. Francis once said, *'For it is in giving that we receive'.* Believe me, his words are true. I have received more blessings in return by being able to give to you."

A sudden noise on the stairs caused Zander to blink, pulling himself from his thoughts to the children rushing down the stairs toward him. Happy, healthy, cared for, loved. Right on their heels came Rosalie, her blonde hair twisted up and wearing a dress that was both demure and made him want to rip it off all at the same time. The years had not diminished what he felt for his wife.

While their children ran circles around her legs, she stepped into his space and placed her hands flat on his chest, peering up into his eyes. He could drown in those eyes and prayed that he was given a lifetime to be able to do so. His own Sleeping Beauty.

"Are you ready?" she asked, her voice soft as her eyes searched his.

"Ready as I'll ever be," came his reply. Calling for his kids, he wrapped his arm around Rosalie, and they walked outside.

Rafe stood in the library of Bellamy Manor, staring out over the perfectly manicured lawn and gardens leading down the hill toward the woods in the distance. He could not see it now but knew that those woods held a small cabin.

For several months, the cabin had been his home when he first met Eleanor. Small, charming, with a large stone fireplace surrounded by built-in bookcases loaded with volumes.

He always smiled when he thought back to that time when they would read together by firelight and then make love, encapsulated in their own little world. He wondered if perhaps life was not simpler then, but as he heard his children rushing into the room, he would gladly take everything they had to give.

Turning, he watched as his oldest chased his youngest around his legs and they laughed, playing their game of tag.

His mind moved back to his childhood when he landed at Miss Ethel's home. He still remembered his parents before the accident that took their lives. He knew he was lucky… he had known a loving home and then landed in another loving home. His life could have been so different if Miss Ethel had not taken his pain and grief, helped him to carry it, and taught him to nurture the memory of his parents by the hours they spent in her rose garden.

As his children carried their game out the patio doors and under the arbor filled with climbing roses, he remembered her once telling him, *"Amit Ray says to focus your energy on the fragrance and beauty of the petals, not on the thorns."*

And so, she had taught him to hold tight to the loving memories of his parents while reveling in the knowledge that he had been given a second family as a child, filled with love. And now, his next family, one that he and Eleanor created together.

"I hope they're not getting their clothes dirty," Eleanor said as she stepped into the room.

He turned and looked at his wife, the dark-haired beauty that held his heart. Smiling as she neared, he pulled her close and peered down into her upturned face. "They're fine," he assured.

She smiled back, her hands snaking up to hold onto his shoulders. "I'm just joking. On a day like today, they might as well play and be happy." Her smile slowly left as she held his gaze. "And you? How are you?"

"I'd rather be out of this suit and working in the yard."

Her lips stayed curved as her gaze moved about him. "Everything has its season."

He understood what she meant and bent his head, taking her lips in a kiss that swept through him to his very core, just as it had the first time he'd ever kissed her. *Will it always be like this? Where Eleanor's beauty tames me, the beast?* The walls did not provide an answer to that question, but as their kiss was interrupted by their children running back into the room, he knew the beauty of their family would always fill him.

Cael stood in his kitchen, sandwiches and snacks packed in bags, and called out that it was almost time to leave. It did not matter how long they would be gone; he knew his children, like him, always needed a snack.

He thought back to Miss Ethel's kitchen counter, always filled with food, and especially after school, always with a platter of homemade cookies. After his mother died, his grandmother did not have it in her to fix snacks for him, and he had relied on his older sister until he landed at Miss Ethel's house.

She had never made him feel guilty for eating, always saying that she wanted him to grow big and strong. At over six and a half feet tall, she had gotten her wish. Actually, she wanted her boys to grow up happy and healthy, and through her love, she had gotten that wish as well.

His oldest son came running into the kitchen, already tall for his age, and spied the food on the counter. "Hang on, buddy," he said. "You just had breakfast, and this is for later."

His son groaned as though he would never have a morsel to eat for the rest of his life, soon joined by his younger son. He looked up as Regina walked into the kitchen, as always taking his breath away. She was tall, built, and with thick red hair that was now tamed into a simple ponytail. From the moment he saw her on the dance floor, she had fired his blood, and those flames had not lessened.

Placing her hands on her generous hips, she looked

down at their sons and pretended to scold, "You just ate!" Hearing their moans, she laughed and handed each of them an apple, telling them that would have to suffice.

As they raced out of the kitchen, she stepped up closer to him, her curves fitting perfectly to his tall, muscular frame. Reaching up to cup his jaw, she murmured, "You look good, Titan."

He laughed and lifted her chin with his knuckle, saying against her lips, "And you look luscious, Red." He kissed her, and his cock twitched as it always did whenever she was near.

She pulled back slightly, holding his gaze, and he could see that there was something on her mind.

"Whatcha thinking, babe?"

She nibbled her bottom lip as her eyes cut to the side for a moment. Sighing, she looked back up at him. "The timing of this might suck, but you know I can't keep a secret from you."

He tilted his head to the side, waiting for her to speak, when she lifted on her tiptoes and kissed him once again. Sliding her lips around his ear, she whispered, "I'm pregnant again."

His heart pounded as he lifted her in his arms and twirled her around, kissing her with all the passion stored inside. "I love you, Red. I love our sons, and I promise to love this baby with all my heart. Girl or boy, it doesn't matter, I just want you and this new life healthy."

She grinned, the same smile she always offered whenever he made a promise. He knew what she wanted him to quote, and he did not disappoint. *"And when I promise something, I never ever break that promise. Never."*

"You know," she said, "you won my heart the first time you quoted Rapunzel to me."

Kissing her again, he said, "You were always my real-life Rapunzel." His kiss was interrupted as their two boys raced back into the kitchen, wanting to know if it was time to leave. Sighing, he knew it was. Walking out to his SUV with his sons running in front of him, his beloved wife now pregnant with their third child and tucked in his arms, he knew he had the world.

Jaxon stepped into the large master bathroom and watched Morgan as she brushed out her long curls before securing them at the base of her neck with a complicated clip. He stepped behind her and bent to kiss the skin underneath her jaw, now exposed. She was as beautiful as the first time he saw her rising from a swimming pool with her hair slicked back and water droplets rolling down her body. Strong, athletic, sure.

Her body was just as amazing now, even after having two children. He sometimes wondered if their children were not part fish as much time as they spent in the swimming pool with her.

Their eyes met in the mirror, and for a long moment, no words were spoken. Just mutual admiration and love flowing between them.

"You look good all spiffed up." Her eyes cast an appreciative gaze over his body.

He straightened his tie. "I figured I'd wait and put the suit coat on once we get there. I tend to get hot, and I hate to sweat in my good suit."

She turned in his arms, her hands moving to his tie which she straightened ever so slightly before placing her palms on his chest. "Do you know how much I love you?"

Wrapping his arms around her, he pulled her in close. "I remember Miss Ethel reading to us boys when we were little. I can still remember the first time she read the Princess Bride and said, *'Do I love you? My God, if your love were a grain of sand, mine would be a universe of beaches.'* That, my beautiful, little mermaid, is how much I love you back."

He kissed her once more, then the sound of their children from downstairs rang out, and she said, "Can you check on them? I'll be right down."

It was an easy request to check on their children, something he did every morning as they woke up, all during the day, and when they slept at night. He now understood why Miss Ethel tucked them in each night, moving around from child to child to whisper something special. He did the same thing.

He and Jayden had started life out rough but landed soft. Now that he was a parent, not a day went by that he did not appreciate Miss Ethel even more, if that was possible.

Morgan descended the stairs, and his eyes traveled from her heeled pumps up her shapely legs, over her curves, to her brilliant smile. Their daughter exclaimed how pretty Mama was, and he agreed. Picking up his youngest, he escorted his family out to the SUV, ready to face the day.

Jayden's twin daughters, petite like Ruby, had ready smiles for everyone. His son, still a toddler, generally had a serious, thoughtful expression on his face. His children's uniqueness constantly amazed him and thrilled him as each day he watched his children grow.

He often thought of how he and Jaxon landed on Miss Ethel's doorstep, trying to fool her by giving their wrong names. He never understood how she instantly knew which was which from the first time they were introduced. But like so many things with Miss Ethel, it defied reason and defined love.

He sometimes thought that if he had never known Miss Ethel, he might not have ever known true love, other than the love he had for his brother. But, because of her, he now understood the love he felt for Ruby and their children.

As he straightened his tie, he walked down the stairs and entered the living room, seeing his children playing together and his wife sitting on the sofa, laughing at something one of them had said. As soon as her eyes lifted to his, he felt the shot straight through his heart, just like always. Her dress was dark red, showing off her pale complexion and wide eyes. She came to her feet and moved to him, her arms instantly surrounding his waist as he tucked her under his chin.

"You're gorgeous, Ruby," he said. Looking over her head to their children, he added, "Everyone's beautiful."

She tilted her head back and accepted his kiss, lifting on her toes so that their bodies were pressed tightly together. As their lips separated, she asked, "How are you doing?"

"I keep thinking of Miss Ethel and all the things she taught me. Mostly about love."

Smiling, Ruby quoted, *"I love you in this way because I do not know any other way of loving but this, in which there is no I or you...'* That was from a book of love sonnets from Pablo Neruda that Miss Ethel gave to me years ago."

He chuckled, squeezing her tighter. "I see Miss Ethel's influence over more than just us boys."

"I think her influence will be felt for many, many years," Ruby said, her lips gently curving.

"I think you're right." Turning Ruby in his arms, he kept her tucked to his side as they stepped into the living room. "You all about ready to go?"

"Are we going to see all of our cousins?" one of his daughters asked.

"Yeah, everybody will be there. All your aunts and uncles and cousins," Jayden replied.

His other girl looked up, her eyes bright. "Daddy, how come everyone will be there?"

Kissing the top of their head, he ushered them onto the porch and toward their vehicle. "Because that's just what we do," came the simple answer. As he closed her door and walked around to the driver's door, he repeated to himself, "Because that's just what families do."

Asher stood in the master bedroom, looking into the mirror hanging on the back of the closet door. He had straightened his tie but continued to fiddle with the collar of his dress shirt.

Penny walked into the room from the master bathroom, her limp barely noticeable, looking every bit as gorgeous as she always did. Her eyes were also on his, and she cocked her head to the side as she watched him tugging on his collar. She moved directly to him, lifted her hands, and smoothed them over his chest. "It looks great, sweetheart."

"I wasn't sure if it hid my neck tattoos well enough," he replied, his gaze moving from her face back to the mirror where he twisted his head back and forth to see if his tattoos showed.

Penny lifted her hand, cupped his cheek, and drew his face back toward hers. "Asher, you're gorgeous. Your tattoos are part of you, and I won't have you worrying about covering them up."

Lifting his brow, he smirked. "Considering I've got them all over my chest and abdomen, I don't have to worry about covering some of them up. I don't think anyone wants me to go to church shirtless."

She laughed, and he loved the sound. Even after all

these years, he was still awed by her strength and perseverance.

She lifted on her toes, pressing her lips as well as her body against his. He took the kiss deeper, angling his head and delving his tongue inside her warm mouth.

"Eeww," came the voice from the doorway. "Daddy's kissing Mommy! That's yucky!"

Breaking apart, Penny rolled her eyes as they both turned toward their son. "One day, boy, you won't think kissing a woman you love to be yucky at all," Asher said.

Penny moved from his arms to inspect their son to make sure he was ready. He looked so handsome in his little suit, and Asher watched as she pulled him in for a hug. His son might protest yucky kisses, but in that moment, he watched his son's face light with love as his mom's arms curled around him.

That simple scene squeezed Asher's heart, knowing he had never known that kind of mother's love until he landed at Miss Ethel's house. She had taken a scared, lonely, abused little boy and made him feel true love, all while giving him a true family.

He remembered clearly the day that Miss Ethel helped him understand the real meaning of family, not what his birth mother had taught him. She had quoted from Mitch Albom, *"This is part of what a family is about, not just love. It's knowing that your family will be there watching out for you. Nothing else will give you that."* It had been easy for a scarred and scared little boy to recognize the difference between his birth family and Miss Ethel's.

And, having been raised with her love, he found it

easy to pass on to Penny and their children. His son, finished with his mother's hug, ran over to Asher and threw his arms around his legs. Asher bent and scooped him up, knowing that one day his son would no longer want that sign of affection. But just like witnessing what he offered Penny, Asher loved the feel of his son's arms around his neck.

Zeke, satisfied with his shirt, tie, and jacket, walked up to Cynthia and asked, "What about my hair?"

She was in the middle of changing purses, taking out what she needed from a big slouchy bag and putting it in a small black purse. She twisted her head and looked up at him, a flare of interest hitting her eyes as she smiled. "You know, baby, I love your hair."

"I just didn't know if I should leave it down or pull it back," he mumbled against her lips as she moved in for a kiss. When he was working in his restaurants or the homeless shelter kitchen, he always had his hair pulled back in a ponytail or up in a bun. Otherwise, it usually hung below his shoulders, wild and free. But, for the event they were going to, he was uncertain.

"I think the most important thing today is that you're comfortable," she said. Her lips curved into a smile again. "I like it down."

That was all the encouragement he needed, and he kissed her lightly once more before sliding his feet into his dress shoes.

"I'm almost finished changing purses, so can you

check on the baby to see if she needs changing before we go?"

Walking into the nursery, he stopped just inside the doorway, the sight of his daughter just waking up always hitting him in the chest. Her eyes moved his way, and she blinked several times before she smiled. That was new… smiling when she recognized him or Cynthia or her older brother.

A smile from one of his children never got old, and he prayed it never would. He wanted to give them the world, but Miss Ethel had taught him the most important thing he had to offer his children and his wife was his love.

Miss Ethel once quoted Dr. Seuss, saying, *"You know you're in love when you can't fall asleep because reality is finally better than your dreams."* It was not until he found Cynthia, and then they had their children, that he truly understood what that meant. Sometimes at night he would lay awake and watch Cynthia sleep before slipping from their bed and moving to the children's rooms to watch them. He could never have dreamed a life so full was doing something as simple as watching his loved ones sleep.

That was one of the many lessons Miss Ethel had taught him as she opened up her heart and home, giving him a mother and brothers to love.

Quickly changing his daughter's diaper, he dressed her in her soft dress and leggings and carried her downstairs where Cynthia and his son were waiting. As they climbed into their vehicle, Cynthia asked, "Is the food ready for afterwards?"

He nodded. "Yeah, we're going to be meeting at the old home, but I'm having some of the Grimm's employees bring the food over. That way none of us will have to worry with it."

While Cynthia snapped the baby into her car seat, he assisted his son into the toddler seat, making sure he was secure. He opened Cynthia's door, and with a quick glance at her ass in the tight dress she wore, he lifted her by her waist to give her a boost into the vehicle. Once she was seated, she shot him a smile that promised a good time that night after the children were in bed.

He leaned forward and kissed her lightly, then walked around and climbed into the driver's seat. Backing out of the driveway, he turned and headed toward the church.

Cas walked out of the workshop and through the back door of his house in the woods, carrying with him the small, decoratively carved wooden cross that he had made. He had it stained so the grains stood out in stark relief.

He remembered bringing Miss Ethel into his workshop several years ago, and she had run her gnarled fingers over the various pieces of wood, quoting Thomas Hardy. *"Two dwellers in a wood, almost every species of tree has its voice as well as its features."*

There was a time when he would not have known what those words meant, but she had spent so much time making sure each of her boys had their own voices, becoming their own men. She had taken the rough, often unloved, ragtag group of boys and turned them into a family while making sure she nurtured each of them individually.

He gently laid the wooden cross on the table before reaching for his tie which he had hung on a dining room chair. He slung his tie around his neck, efficiently knotting it before he looked over his shoulder at Bianca coming down the stairs, holding their baby. Wearing a dress and heels, she had not lost all of her baby weight, and he grinned. Her body was lush with curves, and he loved the softness when he pulled her close.

Her gaze ran over him appreciatively. "Oh, my, Cas, you're as gorgeous as always!"

He bent to take her lips in a kiss. "You've gotta know, babe, you're the one who's gorgeous." He moved to kiss the top of his daughter's head, whispering, "And so are you, little sleepy one."

Bianca held her daughter with one arm but placed her free hand on his chest and said, "I love you. I hope everything goes well today."

"I love you, too, babe. And we're as prepared for today as we can be."

She gave his chest a little pat, then turned and grabbed the large diaper bag. He started to reach for the bag, then remembered the cross still on the dining room table. "I'll be right back," he said and hustled into the other room, picking up the carved cross and tucking it into his suit coat pocket.

Once back in the living room, he took the diaper bag

from Bianca's arms and locked the front door after they walked out. The sun was shining that day, the rays coming down through the leaves in the trees. He and Bianca had made their home in his cabin in the woods, he now devoting his full-time career to furniture making and she still writing her novels.

They lived well off the money they made, and he insisted that Bianca's inheritance be held for their children. At that suggestion, she had smiled and said her father would have loved that idea.

Lucille and Lionel had gone to prison for their attempts on her life and inheritance. Cas, along with his brothers, their women, and Miss Ethel, had kept a close eye on Bianca, but she appeared to have no problems putting their duplicity behind her. Instead, she relished the time she could spend with the women, spent hours with Miss Ethel as they knitted together, enjoyed being with his brothers, and was now building a life with him as his wife and the mother of their baby.

Climbing into their vehicle, he pulled out of their gravel lane, heading to the church in town, his mind filled with what they were facing.

24

Eight SUVs parked outside the church, their passengers unloading. Brothers greeted brothers with handshakes and heartfelt hugs, some with their children's hands clasped firmly in their own. Women hugged each other while cradling babies and toddlers. Children laughed and called out to each other. The men greeted the women, kissing cheeks and children.

Zander approached Cas and said, "Are you ready?"

Nodding, he replied, "As ready as I'll ever be."

The gathering moved up the church's steps, quieting their children as they walked through the doors. It was a small church, and only a few people already sat in the pews. Looking toward the front where the minister waited, the eight men with their women and children in tow, made their way forward.

As they reached the minister, they each nodded before turning to the front pew. There Miss Ethel sat, wearing her Sunday best, smiling with joy and pride.

Standing, she spread her arms wide and said, "Oh, my dearest ones, isn't this a wonderful event?"

Everyone flocked around her, hugs and kisses ensuing. She had not wanted anyone to rush, so she had gotten one of her friends to drive her to the church. It took several minutes for everyone to make sure they had greeted her, the older children immediately going to the woman they considered to be their grandmother, Nanny Ethel.

Finally, everyone had a seat and the gathering filled the first three pews. The minister stood at the front, smiling, and called Cas and Bianca forward. She carried baby Lisa, so named for Bianca's mother.

Cas wrapped his arm around his wife and his baby girl as they stood at the front, heads bowed as the minister prayed. He spoke for just a moment about the meaning of family, his comments poignant as he knew all about Miss Ethel.

"Families are the people we gather around ourselves. Those willing to sacrifice for the children given to their care. As you have been given the most perfect example of motherhood through Miss Ethel, raise your daughter with the same love and care."

The minister finally reached out his hands and held Lisa in his arms. Cas found his breath catching in his throat as he watched the minister dip his hand into the water and bless his daughter's head in infant baptism.

The service was soon over, and he and Bianca eagerly took Lisa, accepting the well wishes and congratulations from everyone present. He had witnessed the same event over and over with each of his seven brothers as they had children, Miss Ethel always in the front center pew. But somehow, experiencing it with his own child had tears running down his face.

As the others circled around Bianca holding Lisa, he stepped to the side to wipe the moisture from his cheeks. A soft but strong touch was felt on his arm, and he looked down to see Miss Ethel staring up at him. Her eyes, now gray, shone with tears of her own.

She reached up and patted his cheek, saying, "I used to say that my greatest joy was raising my boys. But I believe that has now been surpassed by watching my boys find love and raising their own children. You, my dear Cas, have made me a very happy woman, and I'm honored to have you in my life."

He had no doubt that she had given the same words to each of his brothers every time they held the service for their children. But now that it was his turn, her words moved through him, and his tears renewed. Wrapping his arms around her thin body, he whispered, "Thank you, Miss Ethel. For taking me in. For giving me a family. For loving me."

"My dear," she smiled, "George Sand said, *'There is only one happiness in this life: to love and be loved.'* I am a very happy woman." With that, she patted his arm and moved back amongst the gathering.

Bianca sidled up next to him, Lisa tucked tightly into her arms, and said, "I overheard that. And I agree. I am a very happy woman."

With that, Cas bent and kissed Bianca's lips before bending further to kiss his daughter's head.

25

FIVE YEARS LATER

The back yard of Miss Ethel's house was overrun with a huge gathering of people. Zander and Rosalie, Rafe and Eleanor, Cael and Regina, Jaxon and Morgan, Jayden and Ruby, Asher and Penny, Zeke and Cynthia, and Cas and Bianca. Between them, twenty-one children of various ages ran around or sat on blankets.

A large wooden swing set playground had been built to the side, now filled with children. Zander and Zeke manned the grills while the other men kept an eye on the little ones playing. The women hustled back and forth between the kitchen and the tables, continuing to bring food and watching to make sure the children did not sneak any ahead of time.

Miss Ethel sat in the shade, her smile wide as she watched her yard filled with her loved ones.

She felt a hand on her shoulder, as soft as a breeze, and turned to see who was there. George smiled down at her, his fingers giving her a little squeeze. A light emanated from him, ethereal and serene.

His hair was lightly streaked with grey, his eyes still blue. When she first saw him as a teenager, she had thought he was the most handsome boy she had ever met. And she still felt that way all these years later.

He came to her at times… often when she needed him the most. Her boys always thought that she handled things so well, but the truth was she had sometimes been terribly afraid of not being the best mother they deserved. They had such needs, and while she had enough love to give abundantly, she had moments of doubt. George would come to her in dreams, often after she spent time on her knees in the dark of the night.

George would tell her that she was doing what God always intended her to do… share her love.

She occasionally wondered what her life would have been like had he not left her so unexpectedly, but her life was so full that she gave little time to those musings. Life gives and life takes… to question it is futile. Life took her George but gave her the boys.

Smiling up at him, she tilted her head slightly and said, "You come to visit me more often now, my dear."

His gentle smile remained firm as he said, "I miss my Ethel. I like to make sure you still remember me."

"Oh, posh," she chuckled. Her mirth slowed. "You were always the love of my life, George Wiseman. You still are." She hesitated, swallowing deeply before finding the courage to ask, "Am I coming to be with you soon?"

His gaze lifted from hers, and he peered out over the large gathering. Not answering her question, he said,

"You've raised a wonderful family, my sweet wife. You've accomplished so much on your own."

"No," she refuted, shaking her head. "I had a lot of help from a lot of people over the years. And with you and God in my corner, I was able to give my boys the best family. And they, in turn, gave me mine."

His gaze moved back to her and his smile widened. "You always were so generous. Did you know I thought you were the prettiest girl I had ever seen when we first met at the church social? And the sweetest? Even all these years later, you still have my heart."

Her smile widened, and she blushed as she reached up and patted his hand.

"You still have work to do," he finally said. He bent to kiss the top of her head, and she felt her hair move slightly with the breeze.

"You'll come visit me?" she asked, already knowing the answer but finding that she needed to hear his response anyway.

"Oh, my dear Ethel, I'm never very far away. I'm in every breath you take and every beat of your heart. And when it's time… I'll be with you, waiting."

"Nanny Ethel!" came the cry from one of the children. "Can you tell us a story?"

She offered George a tremulous smile, patted his hand once more before he left on the breeze, then turned to the children rushing to sit on the grass at her feet. She clapped her hands in joy and exclaimed, "I always have a story for my lovelies!"

With all of the children gathered around and all of

the adults sitting in a semi-circle behind them, Miss Ethel, with her eyes bright and her smile wide, began.

"Once upon a time…"

Don't miss the next Heroes at Heart
For all of Miss Ethel's boys:
Heroes at Heart (Military Romance)
Zander
Rafe
Cael
Jaxon
Jayden
Asher
Zeke
Cas

AFTERWORD

I have never written a series that has impacted so many people. The emails and messages letting me know that Miss Ethel is the readers' favorite character of all time has warmed my heart. Thank you, Chasity Jenkins-Patrick for telling me that these wonderful men had to be connected. That encouragement gave me the nudge to discover Miss Ethel inside of me and has now allowed me to share her with the world.

ALSO BY MARYANN JORDAN

Don't miss other Maryann Jordan books!

Lots more Baytown stories to enjoy and more to come!

Baytown Boys (small town, military romantic suspense)

Coming Home

Just One More Chance

Clues of the Heart

Finding Peace

Picking Up the Pieces

Sunset Flames

Waiting for Sunrise

Hear My Heart

Guarding Your Heart

Sweet Rose

Our Time

Count On Me

For all of Miss Ethel's boys:

Heroes at Heart (Military Romance)

Zander

Rafe

Cael

Jaxon

Jayden

Asher

Zeke

Cas

Lighthouse Security Investigations

Mace

Rank

Walker

Drew

Blake

Tate (August 2020)

Hope City (romantic suspense series co-developed with Kris Michaels

Hope City Duet (Brock / Sean)

Carter

Brody by Kris Michaels

Kyle

Ryker by Kris Michaels

Saints Protection & Investigations

(an elite group, assigned to the cases no one else wants…or can solve)

Serial Love

Healing Love

Revealing Love

Seeing Love

Honor Love

Sacrifice Love

Protecting Love

Remember Love

Discover Love

Surviving Love

Celebrating Love

Follow the exciting spin-off series:

Alvarez Security (military romantic suspense)

Gabe

Tony

Vinny

Jobe

SEALs

Thin Ice (Sleeper SEAL)

SEAL Together (Silver SEAL)

Letters From Home (military romance)

Class of Love

Freedom of Love

Bond of Love

The Love's Series (detectives)

Love's Taming

Love's Tempting

Love's Trusting

The Fairfield Series (small town detectives)

Emma's Home

Laurie's Time

Carol's Image

Fireworks Over Fairfield

Please take the time to leave a review of this book. Feel free to contact me, especially if you enjoyed my book. I love to hear from readers!

Facebook

Email

Website

Made in the USA
Coppell, TX
28 February 2022